Protection

T. Baggins

For M. F., a lion among men;
and J.M., every day, especially Tuesdays

Protection

New inmates came to Wentworth Men's Prison on Sunday afternoons. They arrived by bus, shuffling single file down the vehicle's steps and into the exercise yard. Gabriel MacKenna knew precisely what awaited them. First they would be marched to the infirmary, where their leg irons would be unlocked and a cursory medical exam would follow. Then the new men would be led down Wentworth's long green and white halls to be kitted out. Jeers and laughter rang through the crisp spring air as the inmates emerged, but Gabriel didn't join in. He stood quietly in the shadow of the watchtower, smoking a Pall Mall and taking their measure.

Gabriel loved the taste of Pall Malls. Convicts detained at His Majesty's Pleasure in April 1936 were issued half an ounce of plain tobacco and a dozen cigarette papers each month, but Gabriel was so skilled at cards, he rarely rolled his own. Wentworth was a modern facility, host to several experimental programs and far removed from its Victorian roots. Gone were the days when prisoners were masked, referred to by number and forbidden to speak to the guards. At Wentworth, the guards were encouraged to mix with the prisoners and provide a wholesome example. Gabriel wasn't sure if gambling with McCrory, Buckland and the other F-block guards had strengthened his moral fiber, but it kept him supplied in Pall Malls. It also kept him informed about recent developments, including the details behind new inmates. None seemed likely to challenge Gabriel's supremacy in Wentworth.

The biggest, a bona fide village idiot named Benjamin Stiles, kept his head down, shooting nervous looks at the gray stone walls and hugging himself tight. Apparently in the village he hailed from, idiots were treated gently. And perhaps Stiles was innocent of the charges, like so many morons condemned by British justice. Or guilty only in a manner of speaking. Either way, Gabriel had no interest in him, because all Stiles had was bulk. To take on Gabriel, a newcomer needed more than mere size.

The last man in line moved slowly, forced to do a hop-step each time the chains pulled tight. He was trying to take it all in – not just the outer wall, erected in 1876, but the watch tower, manned by two guards, and Wentworth itself, old and new. "Old Wentworth" was the original building, four wings radiating off a central area called the Roundabout. A, B, C and D block were there, each cell exactly twelve foot by seven foot. The new prison, constructed in 1910, was a three-story building containing offices, a cafeteria and the infirmary. E, F and G blocks were smaller, but their cells were large enough to house two men.

"Cooper!" bawled Llewellyn, the guard bringing up the rear. "Keep up!"

Gabriel's cigarette halted midway to his mouth. Cooper? Dr. Cooper, the convict McCrory had told him about?

Gabriel stepped out of the watchtower's shadow for a better look. Cooper was no more than twenty-five, with thick ginger-brown hair and wide eyes. Of medium height, he was surprisingly well built for a professional man. The prison uniform fit snug across his broad shoulders and tight against the nip of his waist, the curve of his ass ...

Within hours, the name and story came to Gabriel. Joseph Cooper was a newly qualified doctor convicted of malpractice and gross negligence. Educated at Oxford, Cooper had joined the practice of a well-respected physician in Kent. When Lady Wheaton, wife of Baron Wheaton, went into labor with her first child, Cooper had been entrusted with her care. And when the laboring woman went into distress, Cooper played the hero, attempting to save her single-handedly. He'd confessed as much in writing – his pride, his overconfidence in his own abilities, his hope to be publicly acclaimed by Lord Wheaton. But Jane Wheaton, only twenty-one, had died, and her infant son had died with her. According to rumor, Cooper had attempted an emergency Caesarian, but that, too, had been hopelessly botched. The newspapers had described the scene in loving, lurid detail: Lord Wheaton bursting in to find blood-spattered walls, his young wife slashed open and the infant dead in Cooper's hands.

Lord Wheaton had wanted Cooper charged with double murder, leaning heavily on both the home secretary and the prime minister. But Cooper's physician status shielded him from capital prosecution; the Crown couldn't credibly argue he'd attacked Lady Wheaton, or harmed her through malice. Nevertheless, Cooper had received the maximum sentence for his crimes: eighteen years inside Wentworth, no possibility of parole.

Gabriel saw Joseph Cooper again that evening, in the common time between supper and "reconfinement," as Wentworth's progressive governor, Sanderson, preferred to say. Reconfinement replaced the old term: lockdown. The guard in charge of passing out linens greeted Cooper with passable friendliness.

"C'mon, mate, get yours while it's fresh."

Cooper lifted his chin, smiling back so warmly the guard blinked in surprise. "Ah. Right-o. Thanks very much."

"Talks like a toff, don't he?" Lonnie Parker sounded impressed. During common time he was often at Gabriel's elbow, if not directly beneath his feet.

"Like he's checking in at the goddamn Ritz-Carlton," Gabriel agreed, watching Cooper collect his striped pillow and gray blanket. Cooper's eyes were a very light blue, almost the color of the standard-issue blanket, and long-lashed. He was pale, too, a fellow Celt if Gabriel had even seen one, but pink-cheeked and vigorous, with a healthy bloom to those perfectly shaped lips.

"They say he's a doctor. A bad one." Lonnie loved parceling out bits of gossip he overheard while working in the infirmary, rolling bandages and scrubbing instruments. "Dr. Royal knew all about him."

Birds of a feather, Gabriel thought darkly. He hated doctors in general and Dr. Royal in particular. Gabriel hadn't seen the inside of the infirmary since his last mandatory physical exam, and even then, they'd had to threaten him with birching to make him comply. Corporal punishment was still very much a part of the British penal system. Not even Governor Sanderson was prepared to abolish the practice – public birching against bare buttocks for misdemeanors, an old-fashioned lashing across the back for serious misdeeds. All but the most defiant personalities took the threat seriously. Not even Gabriel would choose the birch over a mere half-hour in Dr. Royal's domain.

"Gabe." Lonnie pressed closer, lips brushing Gabriel's earlobe. "Fancy visiting the library?"

Lonnie didn't want to borrow a book. In fact, Gabriel had never seen the younger man read anything except the cafeteria's daily menu. But the library stacks were good for quick bits of mischief, especially Fiction A-Br, which was tucked in the library's back corner. After three months, Gabriel was already tired of Lonnie, but that glimpse of Cooper – chin lifted, smiling – had primed his pump.

"Go on. I'll meet you."

As Lonnie headed to the library, Gabriel hung back for a judicious interval, asking Tom Cullen to keep an eye on the library's entrance and Bobby Vincent to lurk near the card catalog. F-block men traded such favors all the time, without complaint and never demanding details. Of course, allowing Lonnie to get him off within earshot of Tom and Bobby was mildly embarrassing, yet necessary. To be surprised by a guard, even one like Buckland, who would break up the action but never report it, would have shamed Gabriel far worse.

The stacks had that familiar old scent, a mix of decaying paper, glue and old leather Gabriel had loved since childhood. Leaning against the steel bookcase, Gabriel unbuttoned his fly, closing his eyes as Lonnie knelt before him. Hands drew out his cock, squeezing it with a firm, practiced motion. Gabriel tried to think of Marlene Dietrich – lately the image of her wavy blond hair and those long, perfect legs was his surest route to satisfaction. But after what seemed like forever, Gabriel was there, wasn't even close. There was no firmness in his balls, no rising tension in his lower belly.

Lonnie shifted from hands to mouth, enveloping Gabriel with hot, wet strokes. Gabriel opened his eyes and watched for a bit, then closed them again. True, it felt good – sweet Christ, he was only human, and Lonnie knew his way around a stiff cock. But actually seeing Lonnie sucking him usually did nothing for Gabriel. Sometimes the sight caused a total loss of arousal.

Casting about in his mind, Gabriel thought suddenly of Joseph Cooper – prison uniform taut across his broad shoulders and clinging to that firm, perfect ass. Remembering Cooper's smile, the shine of those gray eyes, the curve of those lips, Gabriel felt his cock jerk. Then it wasn't Lonnie down on his knees, but Cooper, mouth wide, taking every swollen inch. And before Gabriel knew it, release was near.

"Oh," he whispered, imagining Cooper tug, tug, tugging as he sucked the root of Gabriel's cock. Something about the memory of that smile, those long-lashed gray eyes, made Gabriel's asshole clench helplessly. Then he was unloading down the back of Lonnie's throat, coming hard as he imagined sending a jet of white-hot cum into Cooper's belly.

Gabriel walked Lonnie back to E-block. Pretty little Lonnie, a natural victim in Wentworth's harsh Darwinian model, constantly attracted the wrong sort of attention. That night one of the new men, a recidivist named Smyth, was holding court with his old cronies, telling stories about the outside world. Catching sight of Lonnie, Smyth broke off in midsentence.

"Oi! Girlie! You're the first improvement I've seen in this old heap!"

Lonnie kept walking toward his cell as if he hadn't heard. Gabriel moved to Smyth's side. Gabriel was six feet tall; Smyth, a burglar known for crawling into manor houses through cat-flaps and doggie-doors, barely came up to Gabriel's shoulder.

"You're new here." Gabriel smiled.

Smyth rose up on the balls of his feet. "Been on holiday is all. Back now. You're the one is new. Who the fuck are you?"

Gabriel tapped the MACKENNA sewn above his

uniform's left breast pocket. "Not much of a reader? That it?"

Smyth's upper lip curled. From the rapid flush across his cheeks, Gabriel guessed he was a hotheaded little man, desperate to prove himself. "Bloody well pardon me, Irish. I meant to say, who the fuck do you *think* you are?"

"Like it says." In one move, Gabriel dug the fingers of his left hand into Smyth's shoulder while seizing the little man's balls with his right. "MacKenna. Gabriel. Should've got the noose. Got two life sentences instead. That girl," he said, meaning Lonnie, "is mine. All mine. Step out of line and I'll kill you."

Giving Smyth's balls a vicious twist, Gabriel left the little man on his knees. Turning, he made his unhurried way back up to F-block. Dozens of inmates and at least one guard, Buckland, had witnessed the exchange. But the prisoners would never grass. Even Smyth, if questioned, would claim ignorance of who assaulted him. Every convict in Wentworth would rather be known as a coward or a moron than a grass. It was a facet of prison culture that particularly frustrated Governor Sanderson. He had no idea why inmates obeyed that unwritten code, or why guards like Buckland played by the same rules. But Governor Sanderson dwelt in his mahogany-paneled office with a soft chair, a wide picture window and a liquor trolley. He only mixed with the convicts a few times a year, under carefully controlled circumstances. Eight hours a day, five days a week, Buckland lived alongside Wentworth's prison population, good times and bad.

Back in his cell, Gabriel stretched out on the bottom bunk and pretended his cellmate, a flatulent mouth-breather named Owens, didn't exist. Owens was due for release in a month, and was plainly terrified by the threat of freedom. His wife had run off years ago; his children, whom he wouldn't recognize, lived in an East London orphanage. The only sort of work Owens was trained for – old-fashioned blacksmithing, shoeing horses and hammering out crude farm implements – had dried up while he served his time. Gabriel suspected his vacation from Owens would be brief. No doubt the big oaf would endure six months of freedom, commit a second offense to dwarf the first and return to Wentworth for life.

Wentworth's overhead lights extinguished at nine o'clock in autumn and winter, ten o'clock in spring and summer. When they shut off, Gabriel put aside his book – *The Woman in White* – and thought again how useful a handheld torch, like the guards carried, would be. All he had to do was maneuver Buckland or McCrory into wagering one, and sooner or later it would be his. Gabriel hated putting aside a book before he was ready.

As usual, Owens waited until two minutes past lights out to squat over the bucket and take his nightly shit, stinking up the entire cell in the process. Then he clambered into his top bunk with all the finesse of a rhinoceros. Flopping onto his back, he had a wank, mattress springs squeaking as he worked himself up to a fever pitch. Gabriel wouldn't have put up with either from most of the other inmates. But for all his fearsome reputation, Gabriel was slim and compactly muscled, better known for fighting dirty than overcoming men with brute strength. Twice Gabriel's size, Owens had been convicted of beating two men nearly to death over someone else's unpaid loan. As much as Gabriel resented the nightly shit followed by the audible wank, he had the feeling if he took a stand over such inconveniences, he was the one who'd exit Wentworth in a pine box. And that, surely, was the Lt. Governor's reason for assigning Gabriel and Owens to the same cell – so F-block's alpha males could effectively neutralize one another.

Soon Owens was snoring, a long whistle followed by a double rattle. Gabriel hardly registered the sound. That was part of prison life, hearing things after dark, sometimes intimate, often crude. Gabriel's mind was back on Joseph Cooper, tantalized by a new possibility and unable to banish it from his mind. Eventually, he began telling himself it would be a disciplinary action. He couldn't allow a killer of helpless women and children to stroll into his territory, his Wentworth, without showing the little prick who was boss. Besides, Gabriel had earned the indulgence. Gabriel had entered Wentworth with two life sentences round his neck, determined to beat back any man who sought to dominate him and never to be buggered, even if it killed him. Five years later, he'd entered a few uneasy truces – as with Owens – but no inmate had ever cowed him. Nor had one buggered him. The only man to try, a squinty brute named Carl Werth, had forced his veiny, uncut cock between Gabriel's lips. And Gabriel had snapped his jaws shut with all his strength, cracking a molar and biting off Werth's manhood in the process.

Gabriel had been dragged to the infirmary, a grim cluster of black-tiled rooms not renovated since Victoria sat the throne. Werth, borne on a stretcher, was screaming and crying; Gabriel, spitting blood, was furiously denying he'd willingly fellated the other man. Homosexual conduct, though rampant inside Wentworth, was subject to unwritten bylaws, and an inmate ignored the nuances at his peril.

Known homosexuals incarcerated within the British penal system were in immediate and continual danger of their lives. Despised by guards, administrators and inmates alike, such individuals were friendless, shunned as perverts and creeps. Gabriel, who'd been inside only three weeks when Werth tried to rape him, would have slashed his own wrists before letting himself be branded homosexual. And yet Werth, sweating bullets on the stretcher with an open wound where his penis used to be, had been under no pressure to explain himself. Like most dominant men serving a long sentence, Werth had simply picked a presumably weaker male to be his "girl." In Wentworth, being homosexual was an unpronounced death sentence. Yet being like Werth, a prison queer, was merely sinful, no more or less damning than masturbation.

In the bunk above Gabriel's head, Owens let out an

explosive fart. Gabriel pressed his face against his pillow's rough ticking. He wondered how Dr. Joseph Cooper was enjoying his first night inside. Still pretending he was at the Ritz-Carlton?

When Werth and Gabriel were presented to him for treatment, Dr. Louis Royal had been new to Wentworth and the British penal system. Dr. Harper, always calm in a crisis, had started issuing orders, but Dr. Royal had just stood there, taking in Werth's torn flesh and Gabriel's bloodstained teeth with evident disgust. As Dr. Harper arranged Werth's emergency transport to St. George's Hospital, fastening leg irons around the trembling man's ankles, Dr. Royal had examined Gabriel's injured right hand.

In the struggle, Gabriel had dislocated his ring finger and broken his pinky. Dr. Royal assessed the injuries without speaking. Then he placed his hand atop Gabriel's, scarcely allowing his elegant manicured fingers to touch the swollen flesh.

"Men like you make me want to vomit," Dr. Royal had whispered. "Men like you should go directly to the gallows."

Seizing Gabriel's injured fingers, Dr. Royal had twisted them round, crushing the broken pinky and cracking the dislocated ring finger above the knuckle. Maddened by pain, Gabriel had launched himself at the doctor's throat. Six guards were required to pull Gabriel off Dr. Royal, who'd pressed charges the very next day. But the testimony of those guards, including McCrory and Buckland, had tipped the scales in Gabriel's favor. Dr. Royal had been censured for unprofessional conduct and Gabriel had received the lash – not for homosexuality, as he'd feared, but for grievous bodily injury of a fellow inmate. He'd lost his pinky finger, too – infection had settled in the crushed bone – but compared to the hell of thirty lashes, amputation of a minor digit went unnoticed.

Gabriel had borne up to the lash bravely. Not for nothing had he weathered his da's beatings year after year, some deserved, some not. He hadn't pissed himself, hadn't wept, hadn't begged. He still bore the scars across his back – he would until he died – but his silent endurance of the cat-o'-nine tails had made a lasting impression among his fellow convicts. During Gabriel's recovery, Carl Werth had been transferred to Pentonville Men's Prison. So nine-fingered Gabriel MacKenna had inherited Werth's place inside Wentworth, and all had been right with the world.

Except now I'm a prison queer, just like Werth, Gabriel thought, flopping onto his left side in hopes it would prove more conducive to sleep than his right. *Or as near as makes no difference. Why deny it? Why deny what I need?*

Even after five long years of incarceration, Gabriel had never given himself over to the pleasures so many inmates took for granted. He'd entered Wentworth vowing not only to never be buggered but also to never stoop to buggery for his own relief. Yet five years with only rare glimpses of living women had taught him the meaning of blue balls. His ex-fiancée, Mattie, had married some other geezer after two years; the girl he'd seen on the side, Sheila, had marched down the aisle even quicker, but written to Gabriel anyway for a while. Then she, too, had found some better diversion, condemning Gabriel to endless, empty nights. Sometimes he got his hands on a bit of contraband, a French postcard or 'a dirty book, but mostly he was forced to rely on stale memories. Until finally, three months ago, Gabriel had turned to Lonnie Parker and made him his girl.

Lonnie had been sentenced to twenty years for running a grand larceny ring. A lovely young man with bright blond hair, green eyes, and only the faintest shadow of a beard, twenty-three-year-old Lonnie had protested his innocence from day one, swearing he'd fallen in with tricksters and been stitched up. He was too streetwise, too well versed in the lingo of the habitual thief, to be the literal innocent he claimed, but leader of a thieves' network? Lonnie couldn't have masterminded a child's birthday party. Surely that had been obvious to both judge and jury, but His Majesty's justice worked in mysterious ways.

Within days of his arrival, Lonnie had been buggered by his cellmate and raped by G-block's gang of hypermasculine prison queers, the Lovelies. Hollow-eyed, off his food and widely expected to top himself, Lonnie had been too frightened to speak when Gabriel sat down beside him at supper one night. But he'd accepted the offered cigarette, a Pall Mall, and kept it between his lips as Gabriel lit it. After that, Lonnie had been under Gabriel's protection. And Gabriel had been within his rights to ask any payment he wished.

It started with hand jobs. Gabriel, repulsed and aroused by Lonnie's touch, had initially believed hand jobs would be enough. But Lonnie, brimming with gratitude and new life, soon offered to suck Gabriel off, and after the third time Gabriel agreed. Eventually, he'd started kissing Lonnie, surprised by how little the action stirred him. Trying to imagine Lonnie as a woman was impossible; Lonnie was low-voiced and narrow-hipped, with no tits and a point of entry Gabriel didn't like to think about. Once while Gabriel was kissing Lonnie, eyes shut tight as he thought of Sheila, Lonnie pulled out his own cock and pressed it into Gabriel's hand. Jerking away as if scalded, Gabriel had marshaled all his self-control not to slap Lonnie across the face. But Lonnie didn't deserve such brutality. He was only trying to earn his protection by offering equipment Gabriel didn't want.

What if it's not the equipment? Gabriel asked himself uncomfortably. *What if Lonnie's the problem?* Gabriel had never liked stupid or passive women. Why should those qualities be any less off-putting in a man?

Gabriel let himself remember how Joseph Cooper's uniform fit him, that snugness across the shoulders and rear. Not to mention the face. Cooper was beautiful, yet not feminine. As a free man, Gabriel's appetite for sex had been prodigious. Now that he knew he couldn't last another thirty, forty, or fifty years on the occasional hand job or suck off, perhaps it was time to accept masculine beauty? The cock, the balls and an asshole as the only route to satisfaction?

Up in the top bunk, Owens moaned in his sleep, releasing an especially pungent fart. Soon all of F-block would smell like Hell's waiting room. Twenty-two more days, Gabriel told himself. He'd receive the lash for harming Owens or the noose for killing him, and just at the moment Gabriel wasn't in the market for either. Best to bend his thoughts elsewhere, on something worthwhile. Like how to get Joseph Cooper alone.

Judging from Old Wentworth's design, Victorians viewed bathing as something to be done rarely, or only in small doses. The Roundabout's lavatory had just one tub. The inmates of A, B, C and D block used it just twice a year, queuing up naked for the privilege and dunking themselves in the same increasingly gray water. Otherwise, each man depended on his cell's washbasin and flannel to keep clean. A new cake of hard yellow soap was issued every January whether the old one was melted to a sliver or not.

Toilet facilities in both Old Wentworth and the new building were even more primitive. Flushing toilets were reserved for administrators, not inmates. In the yard there was a privy; otherwise they made do in their cells with plain metal buckets, swapping a full bucket for an empty one each morning. Prisoners and guards alike despised "slopping out," as the daily ritual was called. Gabriel had never thought much about it; he'd grown up in a house with nine younger siblings and no indoor plumbing, just an outhouse and a well. But most of the prisoners considered slopping out an institutionalized form of humiliation, and Governor Sanderson agreed. But retrofitting Wentworth with a toilet per cell would be an incalculable expense, something the Home Office would never approve, even if the toilets were installed with 100 percent convict labor. So Governor Sanderson had compromised by giving the new building a communal shower.

The shower's design was simple. A small towel room with cupboards and wooden benches opened into a square, white-tiled room. Showerheads protruded from the walls; the floor was fitted with grated drains. When the brand new inmates, still serving their month of what used to be called "New Convict Isolation" and was now called "Acclimation Time," filed into the towel room, Gabriel was waiting inside.

As Cooper proceeded into the showers, Gabriel spoke quietly to the others. Luckily, Smyth had already returned to the general population, or he surely would have refused to play along. But the new men, eager to fit in and intimidated by Gabriel, each agreed to piss off in exchange for an extra half-ounce of tobacco and a few cigarette papers. Bathing wasn't compulsory at Wentworth – the very first thing Gabriel would have changed, had he been governor – so declining a shower would raise no eyebrows. Only the big man, Benjamin Stiles, refused Gabriel's tobacco, shaking his head until a chocolate bar was offered. Of the seven men whom Gabriel bribed, Stiles was the only one with no idea why he was being asked to leave, or what he was abandoning Cooper to face.

Once the towel room was empty, Gabriel stripped,

wrapping a white towel around his waist. His cock already poked through the gap, thick and purple with rising excitement. Women had always reacted to it with nervous laughter, giggling at how huge and ugly it was. Gabriel never felt insulted. Those same women were soon gasping and spreading themselves wider, riding him with frantic rocking jolts as if afraid they'd never be so perfectly filled again.

Cooper stood beneath one of the far wall's showerheads. The water beat down on his head and shoulders at full blast, steam rising as he soaped himself with the gusto of someone who considered cleanliness next to godliness ...

Gabriel watched. Cooper's ass was firm and perfect. His thighs and calves were surprisingly well muscled, as if he'd done real work in his life. And when Cooper turned around, rubbing his face and scalp beneath the water, Gabriel's belly clenched at the sight of the other man's cock. It was just the right length, all the same width, all the same color. Gabriel, who'd only had one cock in his mouth – the one he'd bitten off – had a sudden impulse to hold Cooper down. To kiss that soft, perfect member 'til it swelled, a luminous white teardrop forming on the head ...

Gabriel stopped, surprised at himself. That wasn't just prison queer nonsense. That was poetic Irish nonsense. Gabriel's own mum had adored poetry, treating herself to a daily orgy of words, and everyone knew how that turned out.

"Oi. Doctor." Gabriel stepped onto the white-tiled floor.

Cooper stepped away from the blast as Gabriel

yanked off his towel, tossing it away.

"No women and children here. Only me."

Cooper stared at Gabriel. Then his mouth hardened. When he spoke, his voice was unexpectedly threatening. "Piss off or I'll knock your teeth out."

"Will you now?" Gabriel felt himself grin. "You and what army?"

Rushing at Cooper, Gabriel collided with the younger man's midsection, knocking him against the wet tiled wall. Cooper struck it with a *whuff*, yet still managed to punch Gabriel so hard he saw stars. With a low grunt Gabriel hit back, slamming Cooper in the gut. The young man made a choking noise as if he might vomit. Then he slid down the wall, head back, both hands clutched to his belly.

Cooper must have been dazed. His thighs were spread wide, pretty cock exposed. The curve of each buttock was plain, a trickle of shower water flowing between them to circle a steel-grated drain.

"Think I'll fuck you like this." Gabriel started to throw a leg over.

"No!" Cooper cried, as much animal denial as human speech. His pupils were dilated, eyes red and desperate. He threw another wild punch at Gabriel, barely grazing his jaw, then two more at Gabriel's chest, clumsy, frantic. Gabriel, ever calculating, waited until he saw an opening, planting his fist exactly where he'd hit Cooper before. This time Cooper fell forward, retching helplessly.

"My third conviction," Gabriel said in Cooper's ear as the young man struggled to control himself, "was grievous bodily harm for biting a man's cock clean off.

Werth didn't die, but it was a very near thing. You know how men are. Attached to their parts."

"Leave me alone," Cooper gasped, trying to scramble up. Gabriel dug hard fingers into the other man's shoulders, holding him in place.

"Look at you. On your knees, ass in the wind, telling me what to do." On one level, Cooper's audacity amused Gabriel; on another, it stoked a terrifying anger. "I'll have you, boy, conscious or no. Brace yourself, let me do my worst, and you'll walk out intact. Keep fighting and they'll carry you to the morgue. With my seed trickling out your dead ass all the same."

"No!" Wrenching free of Gabriel's grip, Cooper struck out blindly. His left hand smacked Gabriel harmlessly in the face. But his right fist slammed against Gabriel's inner thigh, jolting his balls in the bargain.

Gabriel gasped. The pain was nauseating. To be so in need and suffer a blow there almost made his breakfast come up. Only his iron control, all the countless other pains he'd suffered, kept Gabriel from vomiting. And his brush with humiliation made him erupt.

"You fucking cunt!" Grabbing Cooper by the hair, Gabriel slammed his temple against the slick floor. "I'll fuck your ass 'til you're dead!"

Balls still throbbing, Gabriel forced Cooper's legs apart. He wanted to believe the wildness possessing him was righteous anger – a need to punish the bad doctors of the world, to make them pay for their sins. But deep down he simply ached to fuck another human being, to be inside someone again. And not just anyone. Joseph Cooper. Gabriel wanted Cooper because he was beautiful, wanted him and hated him – hated that sublime male beauty that could make him deviate, could inspire such frenzy.

"Oh, God," Gabriel choked, pushing himself between Cooper's cheeks.

The young man groaned, face against the floor, semiconscious. "Please ... no ..."

"Shut it. Shut it or I'll kill you first and fuck you after, I swear it." Gabriel forced himself in deeper, groaning as an orifice tighter than any virgin pussy squeezed him like iron. Sweet Mary and all the Saints, no wonder men gave in to this. No wonder it was mortal sin, punishable by an eternity of hellfire. This made everyday fucking feel about as rare and special as fish and chips.

"Please, God," Cooper sobbed, barely able to get the words out.

Gabriel dealt Cooper another blow. Then while the other man lay dazed, Gabriel pushed himself completely inside. The runoff water turned pink. Cooper's moans changed to little hitching breaths of fear and pain. He was even more beautiful *in extremis*, like a martyr going back to God. Maybe Cooper was a good man. Maybe he'd simply lost his way. But he'd killed a mother and child, stolen a husband's happiness, and he had to pay. Besides, Gabriel was too far gone to stop.

"God forgive me," Gabriel said. His hips rocked faster, finding the rhythm, his manhood locked in that exquisite unyielding grip. Release came too fast, too violently, threatening to shake his flesh off the bones. Gabriel couldn't remember ever coming so hard. For what seemed like a long time, he remained inside Cooper, hating to pull free, hating to let it end.

But practical concerns intruded on Gabriel, as they so often did. Even his favorite guards were only so biddable, and the G-block men would soon arrive, howling for hot water. Time to go.

Gabriel paused to wash his cock. He'd be sore from head to root. Cooper looked worse, curled up on his side like a babe cast too early from the womb. The runoff water had turned more red than pink. Probably he needed stitches. If so, Gabriel hoped Dr. Harper, not Dr. Royal, attended him.

He started toward the towel room. Cooper must have heard Gabriel's footfalls and believed himself alone, because he began to weep. He did so almost silently, chest heaving, tears squeezed from behind closed eyes, hands pressed against his mouth to muffle the sound.

Gabriel watched Cooper sob, unable to pull his gaze away. But he must have decided to turn away because he found himself fully dressed and outside the showers. Hanging about was lunacy; Gabriel had to disappear before a hue and cry went up.

His hands were shaking. Clenching them into fists, Gabriel squared his shoulders and strode unhurriedly back to F-block.

It was three weeks before Joseph Cooper returned from his stay in Wentworth's infirmary. He appeared in the cafeteria around noon just as dinner was served – one of those bland combinations the administrators thought the inmates should be so grateful for, tomato soup and chips.

Gabriel had already known of Cooper's impending return, tipped off by Lonnie, who brought the news with transparent misery. Everyone knew Gabriel had a particular interest in Cooper. As Cooper joined the queue for soup, Gabriel studied him, that new hunger reigniting. Sighing, Lonnie pushed his tray aside.

"Something amiss?"

Lonnie shrugged, looking at the floor as Gabriel studied him. Gabriel was thirty-two. Lonnie, just ten years younger, often seemed as feckless and changeable as a child, so Gabriel frequently addressed him as such. "'Tis a sin to waste food."

Taking a chip off his tray, Lonnie broke it in two and stared at the halves.

"Oi. Lonnie."

Lonnie's gaze came up, blinking away what looked like tears.

"Take note. I still have all my limbs," Gabriel said. "Ten toes and all the fingers worth keeping. I can protect more than one man at a time if I put my mind to it. See if I can't."

Lonnie brightened, sitting up straighter.

"The light dawns, does it? Good. Now eat." Gabriel pushed the tray back at Lonnie, who attacked his chips with fresh vigor. Gabriel watched for a while, amused, before turning to study Cooper again.

He looked good. He wore his prison uniform like a suit, filling it out perfectly. Every ginger-brown hair was in place. His cheeks were close-shaven, no nicks, just a neat sideburn beside each ear. As he moved down the serving line, accepting not only tomato soup and chips but also a helping of rhubarb pie, Cooper kept his chin up, a smile curving those lovely lips. Only the scab on his forehead, the fading bruise at his temple, hinted he hadn't spent the last three weeks on holiday.

For all his quiet confidence, Cooper didn't try to join this faction or that. Instead he carried his metal tray to a deserted table near the guard's post, sitting down and beginning to eat with the single-mindedness of one who wishes to be left alone.

"Hallo." Gabriel settled himself on the opposite bench.

Cooper glared at him, gray eyes hard. "You shouldn't be here. I've given evidence against you."

"Have you now. Poor me. 'Tis a wonder they haven't clapped me in irons. Do you even know my name?"

Cooper's gaze shifted to the top left breast of Gabriel's uniform. "MacKenna."

Gabriel struck a match. Lighting a Pall Mall, he pushed the pack across the table. "I'm Gabriel. And I know for a fact you said you never saw the man who had you. Whatever you are, Cooper, you're no grass. Take a smoke."

"I don't—"

"Take it," Gabriel repeated, voice barely audible yet filled with menace. "If you don't, I'll come across this table and dash your brains on the floor. You know I will."

Cooper reached toward the pack. For a long time he stared at Gabriel, pupils dilated, upper lip curled. Then he lifted the box, tapped it and drew out a cigarette.

"Grand. Put it between your lips, darling."

Cooper went rigid. Slowly, deliberately, he placed the Pall Mall on the table. Gabriel smiled, glancing around the cafeteria to make certain everyone saw he wasn't insulted. Dozens of men looked back. It seemed not a soul had missed the exchange thus far, including the guards. Buckland looked curious; McCrory frowned. One of McCrory's reasons for befriending Gabriel was his once-militant heterosexuality. Seeing Gabriel engage in Wentworth's time-honored courtship ritual wasn't easy for the guard, who looked up to Gabriel almost as an elder brother.

"They tell me you went to Oxford on scholarship," Gabriel said. "Which says to me your mind's ripe for educating. So mark me, Cooper. You are the sweetest piece of ass to walk into Wentworth since before Christ made crackers. I'll bet men have made passes at you since you were – what? Twelve? Thirteen?"

The correct answer was thirteen. Gabriel, a good judge of character, recognized the truth in Cooper's eyes. "Well, you can rest easy now. You're no longer up for grabs. I fucked you in the showers—"

"You *forced*—"

"—and that's debatable ownership. But just now I offered you a cigarette and you took it. Let me light it and you're mine. Meaning you're protected from all the bull-necked, ham-fisted motherfuckers who'd kill you trying to love you. No man in Wentworth will touch what's mine."

"I don't want *you* to touch me." Cooper's voice shook with the force of his loathing. "Not ever again."

Bringing his own cigarette to his lips, Gabriel took a deep draw, exhaling the smoke in the other man's direction. "Sure and you don't. But think on it, Cooper. I'm the devil you know. You've endured my worst. I'm only one man and easy to please. Care to let the G-block Lovelies gang-bang you? How bad will it hurt, taking eight men up that tender hole? Half of them have horse dicks and brains to match."

With a swift intake of breath, Cooper shot a glance at the guards. Two stared straight ahead at nothing. The others – Buckland and McCrory – stood contemplating their shoes.

"They won't help you," Gabriel said softly. "You know I tell you true. I'll help you, I'll protect you, but I'll have payment. Pick up the cigarette. Let me light it. Tell every man in Wentworth you're my girl. I'll go to my grave defending you and expect no more than a kiss before bed at night. Or thereabouts," he added, grinning.

"I'm no girl," Cooper said, lips curling back from even white teeth.

"My boy, then. Or just mine. But pick up the goddamn cigarette before the Lovelies decide to give it a go. Eight against one is hard odds, even for me. I don't mind dying to protect your sweet ass, Cooper, but I'd rather not do it before supper tonight."

With a trembling hand, Cooper seized the cigarette. He held it out, gaze fixed on some invisible point as Gabriel lit it.

"Good. Take a draw. Enjoy the goddamn thing. You a Catholic boy?"

"Anglican."

"Close enough. Suck down the fumes and thank God Almighty you get so much pleasure in this vale of tears." Beneath the table, Gabriel's cock had stiffened the moment Cooper placed the lit cigarette between those perfect lips. It was like a watching an angel tempted into sin – delicious, painful and impossible to witness without suffering almost equally in the process. As Cooper smoked, Gabriel looked at the floor, silently reciting Mrs. Lavin's multiplication tables until his crotch was decent again. Then Gabriel stood, gave Cooper a smile and said, "See you tonight. Remember – I'll expect that kiss."

By the time Joseph Cooper returned to his cell, just minutes before reconfinement, Gabriel had already made himself at home. He had precious few possessions – a Bible from his sister Maureen, a packet of personal letters, and a signed photo from the Marlene Dietrich Fan Club. This last had served him so admirably when it came to his late-night needs; he wasn't ashamed to admit he'd obtained it by writing a fan letter. Marlene, though every inch a woman, had the verve, courage and hardness of a man. Kissing Lonnie's mouth might do nothing for Gabriel, but kissing it while imagining Marlene's flawless legs in those delicate stockings was surprisingly effective.

"What – what are you doing here?" Cooper stopped dead, hands curling around the bars behind him and squeezing until his knuckles turned white. "They told me I'd be alone until a cellmate was assigned."

"And here he is." Gabriel restrained himself from laughing in the other man's face. "Didn't I say I expected a kiss before bed?"

Wentworth's guards, in their infinite, cosmic wisdom, chose that moment to begin reconfinement a full five minutes early. They strode down each long hall in turn, slamming cell doors and locking them tight. Once the all-clear was asked, confirmed and shouted back, the main switch was thrown and the overhead lights snapped off. As F-block went dark Gabriel sprang to his feet, a long-fingered hand closing around Cooper's soft white throat.

"This is where you say yes or you die," Gabriel whispered in Cooper's ear.

F-block's only illumination came from a single battery-powered square, glowing faintly near the ceiling in case of emergency. The light bounced off the cell's shaving mirror, revealing Cooper's compressed lips and wide, desperate eyes.

"Yes," he breathed. "Just kill me first. Do anything you like, but kill me first."

The plea lodged in Gabriel's stomach like lead. The damned fool was serious. Cooper's pulse beat frantically beneath Gabriel's fingers like the wings of a trapped bird, but his voice was steady.

"Jesus, boy." Releasing the younger man, Gabriel pushed him onto the bottom bunk. Dropping down beside him, Gabriel caught Cooper's head in the crook of his arm, as he might have done to a younger sibling. Pulling Cooper close, he planted a kiss on the other man's forehead, then let go.

"One kiss paid up. You've earned yourself a quiet night," Gabriel said, feeling in his top breast pocket for cigarettes and matches.

Cooper sucked in his breath, staring at Gabriel. The look in his large gray eyes was hard to take.

"Have one." Gabriel shook a Pall Mall out of the box.

Looking like he didn't know what else to do, Cooper took it. He held it steady as Gabriel lit it. Then Cooper's eyes brimmed over and he began to weep, gaze downcast, tears forming and dropping down each full white cheek.

"Oh, for Chrissake," Gabriel muttered, looking away. "Some wrongs can't be undone. There's no going back, only forward. Don't sit there bawling. It won't bring that poor woman back to life, nor her babe."

"I didn't—" Cooper began, and stopped himself. He made a sound more like choked laughter than tears. "It doesn't matter. God knows it won't matter to you."

"Perhaps not. I've never cared for doctors and that's a fact. But if you're innocent, go on," Gabriel said. "Tell the tale. Mind you, every man inside is innocent. I'd find a guilty man's story more diverting."

Cooper mastered himself. Drawing in a double lungful of smoke, he shook his head.

"You're sure? Confession and the soul. You know what they say."

Cooper shot Gabriel a sudden, vicious look. "I didn't kill Jane Wheaton or her baby. I did my best to save them."

Gabriel didn't throw the details he'd already heard in Cooper's face. In Wentworth, the correct response when a convict told his story was to listen. Even if it was all bollocks, even if anyone who'd scanned a newspaper in the last ten years knew the real story, the only proper reaction was to listen. The judge, the jury, society at large – all three entities had already weighed in on what was true and what was false. The last thing a man inside needed was another inmate calling him a liar.

"You do know I'm listening?" Gabriel prompted at last.

"The thing is, I *wanted* to go to Findley," Cooper said suddenly, as if Gabriel might argue the point. "I was over the moon to join a physician as distinguished as Dr. Pfiser. I had other offers but never considered them." Cooper put the cigarette to his lips. "God knows where I'd be if I had. Not here, that's for damn sure."

Striking a match, Gabriel lit a Pall Mall and waited.

"It started fine. I liked Dr. Pfiser. He was so – encouraging. Never tried to take the mickey, never corrected me in front of patients. Even when he disagreed, he only said, 'That approach doesn't work for me,' or 'I've had no luck with that treatment.'

Never what I expected – 'Don't argue, I'm a well-known physician and you're a nobody who only saw the inside of Oxford because of a scholarship.'"

Gabriel, who'd finished school at thirteen to learn his trade, carpentry, was more curious about university and the scholarship process than Cooper's relationship to Dr. Pfiser. But now was hardly the time to say as much.

"Dr. Pfiser let me work independently more often than I expected, especially at night or on weekends." Cooper looked sidelong at Gabriel. "I should have been suspicious. But when you come out of training, after being second-guessed and watched like a hawk at every turn, it's a great feeling, being the bloody physician. Not Cooper the student but Dr. Cooper, thank you very much." He gave a bitter laugh. "So, yes. During the trial, the Crown mentioned my hubris. My overweening pride. And I guess there was some truth to that point."

Gabriel thought of Dr. Bekins, who'd botched his little brother Robbie's fractured leg, setting the bone so crookedly the boy healed with one limb two inches shorter than the other. Dr. Bekins was a learned man; no one in the old neighborhood disputed that. He was wise about breeding women and colicky babes. But when he'd been at the laudanum, he made mistakes, and patients like Robbie MacKenna had to live with the results.

"Nights and weekends, you say? A family man," Gabriel said. "Or a drunk."

"A drunk." Cooper stared straight ahead into the darkness. "If he'd let me handle Jane Wheaton's labor alone it would have been all right, I think. But he didn't dare. Dr. Pfiser was a personal friend of Lord Wheaton. So when Dr. Pfiser turned up with a red nose and a booming laugh, I ..." Cooper took another deep drag off his cigarette. "I didn't speak up. Didn't steer Dr. Pfiser away from Jane's bed and say I smelt the whiskey on his breath. Didn't warn Jane or Lord Wheaton. I knew my place and kept my mouth shut. That was my real crime. Perhaps that's why God put me in here. If there is a God."

"Oh, there's a God, rest assured of that."

Cooper looked at him with such naked surprise, Gabriel felt warmth rise in his cheeks. Since taking his pleasure in the showers – he wouldn't call it rape, it was just the way of things at Wentworth, what dominant men did to weaker ones – Gabriel had assured himself it was only another sin of the flesh. Now, sitting beside the other man, submitting to that stare, a suspicion crept into Gabriel's mind. Perhaps no matter what Cooper was, it didn't give anyone the right to use him against his will. Not even if he sacrificed pregnant women at the full moon and ground their bones for his bread.

"I didn't proclaim myself a godly man. I only said there is a God," Gabriel snapped, looking away. "So the doctor turned up drunk and you knew it. Go on."

"Dr. Pfiser took charge of Jane's labor. She was pained, of course, and he kept saying she was only afraid, that nothing was truly wrong. All the Wheaton heirs had been born at Wheaton Manor and Jane wanted to preserve the tradition. The boy was already named – John Carothers Sergeant Wheaton. His

christening gown and silver cup were laid out."
Cooper's eyes shone. "Dr. Pfiser was confident, half-
asleep in his chair, but I was concerned. Jane's color
was bad. Her urine smelled of sugar and her lower
legs were swollen. Have you heard of diabetes?"

Gabriel shook his head.

"It's deadly in children and pregnant women.
Sometimes it doesn't present until a few weeks before
labor. Dr. Pfiser missed the signs. But that could
happen to any doctor," Cooper added. "The point is,
once we realized Jane's condition, labor at Wheaton
Manor was too dangerous. She needed transport to
hospital right away. I told Dr. Pfiser as much. He said I
was a good lad, but green as grass and dead wrong. To
disrupt Jane's labor, to anger Lord Wheaton, would be
the unmaking of my career. And that," Cooper sighed,
swiping at his eyes, "that frightened me. So I held my
peace."

Gabriel frowned. So far Cooper had confessed to
two misdeeds, neither of which were actionable in
British courts. As the supervising physician, Dr. Pfiser
carried the liability for both. Gabriel shifted,
unsettled, as if danger crouched at the very edge of
his peripheral vision.

"When things went bad, they went bad all at once,"
Cooper continued. "Jane's pulse turned thready. She
started gasping. And the baby presented placenta first.
That meant Jane would bleed to death, no doubt. She
was already hemorrhaging fast. Outside of a hospital
there was no way to save her life, and if we wasted
time transporting her, the baby would die, too. There
was nothing left to try but a Caesarian." Cooper

looked at Gabriel. "Do you know what that is?"

"How Julius Caesar was taken from his dead mum's belly."

"Yes. Dr. Pfiser had been dozing. He woke up sober, for the most part, and frozen, completely at a loss. I opened his black bag. Pulled out the surgical instruments. Jane was dead, or as near as made no difference, so I performed the Caesarian. I'd just pulled the baby free when Lord Wheaton burst in."

Gabriel could imagine the scene all too easily. He saw a posh bedchamber, a four-poster with old-fashioned bed curtains, the ancestral site of consummations, conceptions, births and deaths. He saw a young mother, dead. And blood everywhere, soaking the bed linens, sprayed on the walls, spattered on the motionless woman and Cooper alike.

"Was it alive?" Gabriel asked, meaning the infant.

"Barely. Lord Wheaton slapped the baby out of my hands. He was wild over the sight of – of Jane laid open that way, viscera exposed, covered in blood. He struck me so hard, I fell and lost consciousness. When I came around, the baby was dead." Stubbing out his cigarette, Cooper tossed down the dog-end and wiped his eyes. "And Lord Wheaton had summoned the constables."

"But you told your story, didn't you?"

"No one asked. Dr. Pfiser told me to go back to my room above his surgery. Said we'd discuss it in the morning. I didn't sleep that night, but not out of fear. I was too foolish to be afraid." Giving a little laugh, Cooper accepted a new cigarette from Gabriel, allowing the other man to light it. "I was sad over the loss of our patients. Not guilty. Sad.

"And so." Putting the Pall Mall to his lips, Cooper drew in another double lungful as if he couldn't get enough. "Next morning, in comes Dr. Pfiser. He's stone-cold sober, more serious than I've ever seen him. Hands shaking with the DTs. You know about those?"

"Delirium tremors," Gabriel said, biting back a smile. "I *am* Irish, if you didn't guess."

Cooper almost smiled back. Then wariness returned to his eyes. "Well. Dr. Pfiser called me into his office. Took out vellum writing paper and a fountain pen. Showed me how terribly his hands shook. He couldn't have written clearly if it meant the firing squad. 'I need you to take down my words,' he told me." Cooper closed his eyes. "And I did. God help me, I did. Word for word. How Dr. Pfiser felt sure he could manage any birthing complication. How he craved Lord Wheaton's patronage. How he shunned all assistance and caused a mother and child's death."

Gabriel caught his breath. He saw it again, the showers, Cooper beneath him and crying out to God for mercy. What had Gabriel told himself? That a bad doctor deserved what he got?

"Dr. Pfiser stitched you up."

"Yes. I'm not sure he meant to, not at first," Cooper said. "Maybe he did. But at some point, Dr. Pfiser realized the confession had been written just as he dictated it, in the first person. A constable came round to arrest me next morning. Said he had a confession in my own hand, a witness – Lord Wheaton – and my own mentor Dr. Pfiser ready to give evidence against me. At first I thought the truth would out. Isn't that what we're taught, growing up? The truth will out?"

"Shakespeare didn't know everything," Gabriel muttered. Cooper's story sounded authentic. Worse, it felt authentic, in the hidden chambers of Gabriel's heart. Educated at Oxford by benefit of scholarship and lacking family connections, Joseph Cooper had found himself at the mercy of a well-respected man and paid the price. Two hundred years ago he would have been strung up on some convenient tree branch for his trespasses. Nowadays he was buggered by the British justice system and sent to Wentworth to marry the man with the most cigarettes.

Which is me, Gabriel thought, ever aware of his tobacco stash, the currency of his world. *Poor trusting bastard who never committed a crime at all. And I reamed his ass like he fucked an entire girls' academy.*

A memory returned to Gabriel, something he'd never confided to anyone. An Easter Sunday when he was six years old and his grandmother had surprised him with a fuzzy yellow duckling. Gabriel had been enchanted. He'd adored the duckling's softness, its orange beak, its intelligent black eyes. For half the day he'd fed it, carried it, talked softly to it. Then the MacKennas had gathered for the afternoon meal. Afterward, six-year-old Gabriel had forgotten his duckling. Caught up in some impromptu game with the other boys – jumping over the back step while slamming the door – he hadn't expected the duckling to dart into the kitchen at the wrong moment. Gabriel, the most vigorous player, had slammed the door on the duckling's neck.

He'd cried and cried until his Da, impatient with weeping girls and infuriated by weeping boys, had threatened to peel the skin off his ass. Choking back his tears, Gabriel had prayed for God to heal the duckling. Gabriel had never meant to hurt it; he would have gladly maimed himself in penance. It didn't matter. The duckling had died and Gabriel's Da had made him bury it, saying, "Boy, you're too great a fool to be entrusted with any living thing."

"Oh, Christ," Gabriel muttered, seeing Cooper curled up and weeping on the shower floor.

"Go ahead." Cooper sounded defiant.

"What?"

"Call me a liar. Isn't that what you said? Every inmate claims innocence?"

Gabriel finished his Pall Mall, dropping the dog-end and grinding it beneath his heel. "When I came here, I said I'd never turn prison queer. I bit off Carl Werth's dick and that was the last of any man trying to force me. But turns out that was only half the battle. You can only imagine fucking women for so long before your body needs relief. So I took a girl – Lonnie, the blond from the infirmary. You know him?"

Cooper nodded.

"Pretty lad. Brains of a gnat. I never did have him," Gabriel said. "Was saving myself, don't you know, like a good Catholic boy awaiting the altar. Awaiting a man who deserved what he got. So I could fuck him into next year and not give a damn what it did to him. And being the sterling judge of character I am,"

Gabriel forced a laugh, "I picked the only innocent man this godforsaken place has ever seen."

Cooper's gaze dropped. He hugged himself, trembling, fighting back more tears with all his strength.

"Cooper. Joseph. Did – did I hurt you so bad?"

The twist of those red lips was answer enough. Gabriel blew out a sigh. Of all the sins he'd committed, venal or mortal, when he was most ashamed, Gabriel remembered that duckling's neck, crushed by a slamming door.

"Fair enough. Joseph," Gabriel said, wishing the other man would look at him. "Some wrongs can't be undone. I wronged you in the showers. I know that now. I'll never use you that way again. But we can start over as cellmates. I meant what I said about protecting you, Joseph. I—"

"Joey."

"What?"

"My name. It's Joey." The younger man let out another bitter laugh. "You've had everything else from me. Might as well have that, too. Everyone calls me Joey."

"Joey." Before he knew he would do it, Gabriel tilted the other man's chin up and pressed their closed lips together. It was just as he'd fantasized – an electric shock, a jolt from his mouth right to the tip of his cock. But the kiss was one-sided. Joey's lips didn't part. His whole body went rigid, eyes shut tight as if in pain.

"Joey." Gabriel pulled back. "Look at me."

Joey obeyed. Gabriel saw the other man's eyes in

the mirror-reflected light. They were blank with terror.

"Joey," Gabriel said again, trying to curtail the emotion in his voice. "What I did in the showers won't happen again. I mean it. But the hard fact is, I'm only human. The price of protection is simple. You have to let me touch you. Kiss you. Not every time the lights go out. Not every night of the week. But – enough."

Joey didn't react. Didn't agree. Didn't resist. Looking into those wide gray eyes, Gabriel had the sudden suspicion the other man was fading, slipping away.

"Joey!" Gabriel shook the other man until he jerked free.

"Stop!"

"It's no good if you go away inside." Gabriel knew he had no right to be angry or frustrated, but he preferred both sensations to abject shame. "When I touch you, when I kiss you, you have to know it's me."

Joey covered his face with his hands. He had nothing left to give, Gabriel realized. If he pushed any harder, the younger man might break altogether.

"Away with you."

"W-what?" Joey asked, returning from far away.

Gabriel pointed at the top bunk. "Tonight's kiss is paid up. Away with you. And not another peep 'til morning."

S ince his realization at age fifteen that he would be
a physician, Joey Cooper had read everything he
could get his hands on concerning anatomy, biology
and pharmacology. But after his sentencing, he'd
given away most of his possessions, including his
science books. As for the prison library's nonfiction
stacks, he avoided them. Daily life held enough bitter
reminders. But unable to survive without books, Joey
had thrown himself headlong into fiction, choosing
novels set in remote times or places. Within two
weeks he'd read *David Copperfield*, *The Last of the
Mohicans*, *Cimarron*, *The Sea Hawk* and *The Good Earth*.

"Hard road for those Chinks," Gabriel had
commented when he saw Joey with *The Good Earth*.
"My grandmother used to say it's no life fit for pigs,
being a lass. After reading that, I think she nailed it."

Joey hadn't known how to reply. Whatever traits
he'd imagined in Gabriel, compulsive reading wasn't
among them. During those early days Joey never
spoke to Gabriel unless he had no choice. But
protracted silence during the hours of confinement
was hard to bear. And Gabriel was surprisingly easy to
talk to, quick-witted and intelligent. More than
shrewd, as Joey first assumed, Gabriel was self-
educated in many areas. He knew the Bible like a
seminarian, quoting it chapter and verse, and could
recite several poems from memory.

"Ah, but I'm a man who likes the sound of his own
voice," Gabriel said when Joey was startled by his
word-perfect rendition of "The Tyger." "A poem's no
poem at all 'til you deliver it with an Irish lilt."

Joey's first two weeks under Gabriel's protection

took some getting used to. Few inmates spoke to Joey without first receiving a silent assent from Gabriel. No liberties, not even joking offers or lascivious remarks, were tolerated. One day a G-block Lovely named Petrocelli had offered Joey "something sweet to suck on." Before Joey could decide if he should feign deafness or hurl back an insult, Gabriel steered Petrocelli to one side, talking quietly to the man while Gabriel's F-block cohorts hovered just out of earshot. To Joey's relief, no physical violence ensued. But it was a very near thing. White with fury, Petrocelli had shambled off. Then Gabriel reappeared at Joey's side with fresh perspiration on the back of his neck and damp patches beneath each armpit.

"What did you say to him?"

"Never you mind." Gabriel sounded unconcerned. "Fetch your supper and think no more on it."

The story of Gabriel's conviction came to Joey in multiple forms, none of them dovetailing sufficiently explain why Gabriel was serving two life sentences, yet hadn't gone to the gallows. Joey was curious, yet refused to ask. Asking was expected. Inside Wentworth, asking was the universal connection: hearing a man's story of how his personal liberty had been lost, squandered or in Joey's case, stolen. But Joey couldn't make that ritual gesture. The moment he asked Gabriel how he'd come to Wentworth, he might as well have declared it was no hard feelings between them, water under the bridge, a bad moment in the showers and best forgotten. And Joey wouldn't do that. It was one thing, answering a direct question about a novel, or a meal, or who would shave first. But the idea of behaving as if he and Gabriel were friendly, much less friends, made Joey want to jerk the blade out of a safety razor and open his own wrists.

And maybe he'd do that before long, anyway. But not just yet.

Joey, expected to sit beside Gabriel during common time, learned to endure the hand on his knee, the smiles, the quick kiss when the guards' eyes were elsewhere. Joey had thought it over endlessly, weighed the cost and decided in order to survive Wentworth, he'd have to accept conditions that would have been unbearable in his former life. After the rape – except he couldn't call it by that word, it made him feel too weak; inside his head he simply called it *what happened* – Gabriel's little ways of publicly declaring ownership seemed small indeed. Joey had needed four sutures after what happened. Then the first time he shit he burst two and had to have them redone. The humiliation of lying on his belly and letting Dr. Harper repair his intimate injury had pained Joey almost as much the memory of Gabriel forcing himself inside.

"You're too pretty for your own good," Dr. Harper had said, stripping off his gloves and tossing them in the rubbish bin. "Let me give you a piece of advice, Cooper. Next time it happens, bear down instead of clenching tight. I don't enjoy putting in these sutures any more than you enjoy receiving them."

Dr. Harper hadn't meant to be cruel. Neither had he meant to be kind. He was simply imparting information. That first night locked in a cell with Gabriel, Joey had been too shell-shocked to think rationally. But afterward, the logic was simple. The most dangerous man in Wentworth had offered him protection. Joey would not be beaten, raped or killed by the other prisoners. Gabriel had even promised not to revisit what happened, but on that score, Joey didn't believe him. Sooner or later, Gabriel would expect all the sexual repayment Joey could give. Still, the conclusion was obvious: appease one man, remain alive and uninjured. Or anger that man, make an enemy of him and take on all of Wentworth in the bargain.

To Joey, the greatest irony was, if it hadn't happened, if he'd met Gabriel during common time and received the exact same offer, he probably would have accepted. Joey had never been squeamish about sex. And given all the male advances he'd fought off in his boyhood – including the vicar, the green grocer and a professor of English literature – homosexuality was no foreign concept. Joey had long ago decided if he were ever seriously tempted, he'd try it. But there had always been plenty of girls available to keep him busy. And the men bold enough to try and seduce him were much older, convinced they could buy him with fine dining, liquor and gifts. Joey had felt sure any real temptation would come from someone close to his own age, well built and attractive. And if not for what happened, Gabriel would have fit the bill.

Gabriel was six feet tall, compactly muscular and handsome. That was a surprise, that Wentworth's resident devil could look so angelic when he willed it. His dark brown hair was always neat, never overdue for the prison barber. His hazel eyes could be soulful or soulless, depending on his mood. Gabriel's working-class background, coupled with his strong native intelligence and adoration of the English language, made him all the more compelling. Once upon a time, Gabriel would have been exactly the sort of man Joey might have experimented with, even made love with. But after what happened ...

Until that morning in the showers, Joey had never thought of himself as a coward. He'd grown up fatherless in a village that never let him forget it, taking odd jobs to supplement his mother's income as a laundress. Sometimes the other children teased him, throwing his natural father's name – Lionel Coates – at him, calling Joey a bastard and his mother a whore. It didn't help that Joey grew up so closely resembling Mr. Coates's daughter, Virginia, they might have been twins. The similarity led to a fresh line of harassment – village children pretending to mistake Joey for Virginia, asking why he was in trousers instead of a frock. During his early life Joey developed a knack for sensing which insults should be ignored and which required a rebuttal or a swift physical response. Decent with his fists, he also learned there were worse things than being knocked about, and that friendships frequently arose from scuffles. By his teens Joey was well liked throughout the village. No one teased him about his natural father or his pretty face anymore. And for his part he learned to hold no grudges, not because he wasn't tempted but because they were utterly without value.

But in the showers Joey had failed to defend himself. Failed to keep from screaming, begging, weeping. Dr. Pfiser and the courts had taken everything external from Joey, but Gabriel had taken everything internal – his optimism, his self-assurance, his belief that no matter how bad things got, he could cope. Just the thought of Gabriel touching him made Joey tremble. Being locked with Gabriel in their cell at night, aware of his presence on the bottom bunk, was torture. The first two nights Joey had hardly slept. Could he remain still for Gabriel, endure whatever happened without retching?

But the first week stretched into the second, and still nothing happened. Gabriel never went into the showers until Joey was done, though he lingered in the towel room to be sure no man tried anything. They ate together, smoked together and gradually began discussing books together. Those rituals grew more and more familiar. But every night Joey climbed into his bunk in his prison-issue pajamas and lay on his back, staring at the ceiling and wondering if this would be the night. And every morning he awakened as the overhead lights snapped on to find Gabriel up and already shaving in front of the cell's small rectangular mirror.

Often Lonnie turned up at their table during supper. From what Joey could deduce, Lonnie was still Gabriel's, though sexual activities between them had ceased. Yet Lonnie didn't seem jealous of Joey. He was a happy-go-lucky sort, cheerful and frequently idle, except for his mouth.

"Do you miss it?" Joey asked Lonnie one night over supper. Gabriel had gone off to roust the gang taunting Benjamin Stiles. The big man couldn't abide raised voices and frequently found himself backed into a corner, the candy bars he bought in the commissary stolen away.

"Miss what?"

"You know," Joey said softly, making certain no one else heard. He'd never met a man willing to admit to homosexuality. Even the men who'd tried to seduce Joey denied it. There was always an excuse – special circumstances or some fleeting appetite. "Being Gabriel's only lover."

"Ah. Well. I suppose." Using his spoon, Lonnie heaped his mashed potatoes into a hill. "Gabe's my sort in lots of ways."

"Your sort. So you were ...?" Joey glanced around surreptitiously. "Homosexual before you were incarcerated?"

Lonnie's head jerked up. "Oi. 'Course not." The denial must have sounded unconvincing even to him, because he added in a suddenly accusing tone, "Why, were you?"

"No." Joey smiled. "I was all set to get married. The girl said yes, the ring was purchased, the church was engaged. Then my life fell apart. But I didn't mean to upset you," he added, resisting the impulse to place a friendly hand atop Lonnie's. The nuances of Wentworth's prison culture were still strange to Joey – God knew what meaning such an otherwise innocent gesture might contain. "I'm merely curious. To know if my turning up here has – well, caused you any grief, I suppose."

Lonnie chuckled. "I do love the way you toffs talk. And if you really want to know," his eyes sparkled, "I weren't exactly what you'd call a *virgin* before I got sent up. But the geezers round here don't want to hear that. Think they're all proper men, hot for pussy or nothing." Lonnie pronounced the last word "nuffink." "Six months later those same geezers are bending me over, going to town like they're riding a thoroughbred. But I'm the dirty pervert 'cause I tried it of my own free will. They think they're better than me 'cause they was driven to it."

"Gabriel says he was driven to it."

"I know." Lonnie glanced around, then leaned across the table, whispering, "But he knows about me. Knows I was queer when I was outside, and never beat or cursed me. He protected me all the same and still does, even now that you're here."

"But have I done you a bad turn?"

Lonnie shrugged, flattening his mashed potato hill into a plain. "Told you. I like Gabe. But I couldn't make him happy. Maybe you'll have better luck."

Joey thought about that. Across the cafeteria, Gabriel was prodding Stiles, still crying, through the food line, forcing him to select meat and vegetables as well as pudding. The convicts who'd tormented the big man had disappeared. They were unlikely to try it again, at least in Gabriel's presence. Gabriel was treated with friendly respect or overt fear by almost everyone, but among the inmates he seemed to have no friends.

Of course not, Joey thought. *Most of them are mentally subnormal or sociopathic.* Their only pursuits were physical exercise, smoking and cards. Gabriel's intellectual curiosity was alien to them. And he could only win so many games of poker. Afterwards, his restless mind would seek fresh stimulation, at least during those hours he wasn't using his carpentry skills toward Wentworth's ongoing renovation.

Joey had assumed that when it came to work detail, he would be sent to the infirmary, but instead he found himself assigned to B-block's overhaul. Governor Sanderson, emboldened by the use of British prison labor to improve roads and dig tunnels, intended to completely rebuild Old Wentworth over the next several years. Gabriel, as Wentworth's only skilled craftsman, a master carpenter, was indispensible to the project. Joey was just another pair of hands, one of over fifty inmates supervised by an architect, an engineer and the guards.

Despite the tools at hand – picks, shovels, hammers, ropes, pulleys, large S-hooks and trowels – the outbreaks of bad behavior had been few. Many inmates seemed to relish hard physical labor, particularly when they could see the fruits of their efforts rising around them. And corporal punishment loomed for any man caught misusing or stealing a tool.

Joey and four others had been set to bricking-in the walls of B-block's new office. Joey alternately mixed mortar and trowelled it into place as the others laid bricks and wiped away globs of oozing mortar. By afternoon, two walls were up. Then the engineer swept through, noticed their progress on the third wall and demanded they stop at once. The specs for a window space had been completely overlooked.

The guard in charge of Joey and the others turned

belligerent, insisting the plans were unclear and no one could have interpreted them properly. More progress that afternoon looked unlikely – the guard was digging in his heels and the engineer was fit to be tied. So Joey and the others had sat down within the shelter of two and a half walls, smoking and laughing as they speculated on how they'd finally be directed to continue.

"Cooper! Bet you can read better than Bynum," one inmate said, meaning the guard who'd misread the plans. "Why don't you volunteer to supervise us?"

Joey smiled. The F-block men were easier with him now, occasionally calling out greetings or stopping to pass the time of day. But Joey recognized a challenge when he heard one.

"If you chaps nominate me, I'd be honored." Joey put on an impossibly posh accent, the sort of enunciation that gave "Shakespeare" four syllables. "But the governor will jolly well have to pay my price, won't he? Is a month's furlough and a case of bubbly too much to ask?"

Laughter and smiles all around made Joey feel almost normal again, back in his home village instead of this nightmare. Then Paulie Jensen turned up.

Paulie was E-block's strong man. Blond-haired and squat, he had an overdeveloped chest and long arms like an albino gorilla. As with many of Wentworth's lifers, Paulie seemed almost supernaturally attuned to the guards' movements. Small pockets of unsupervised mirth drew Paulie like a shark to bloody waters.

"I've been watching you, Cooper," Paulie told Joey,

looking him up and down hungrily. "You're too sweet for MacKenna. His dick tastes like Lonnie Parker's shit, don't you know that?"

"Spit it out, then." Joey didn't stand up, but all his muscles tensed. The visceral response came as a relief. True, Gabriel terrified him. But when it came to normal men, normal threats, he was still the Joey Cooper he'd once relied on. "And while you're about it, piss off."

Paulie's eyes widened. "Stand up and say that."

Joey stood up. When Paulie lunged for him, slow and untrained, Joey caught Paulie's short legs in a wrestling hold and pulled them both down. Then, as if on the mat at Oxford, Joey jerked Paulie's left arm behind his back. Even as the man grunted, unable to break free, Joey gripped Paulie's lower half in a scissor hold.

"Give," Joey warned. "Give or I'll snap it, swear to God."

Something hard connected with the side of Joey's face. He let go of Paulie's arm and legs. It took Joey a second to realize he'd been struck by a glancing kick. The wet warmth on his upper lip was blood. Head still reeling, Joey felt himself hauled up by two of Paulie's crew, spun roughly around and bent over the half-bricked wall. None of the F-blockers were there. No one had stuck around to defend him.

Still dazed by the kick, Joey felt his trousers pulled down. His shorts were yanked to his ankles. He tried to scream but couldn't – two men held him in place while an apelike hand clamped over his mouth. Joey's heart beat wildly against his ribcage, blood roaring in his ears as Paulie rubbed up against him. It was happening again. Joey was bare-assed, helpless, *it* jabbing his inner thigh and about to—

"Paulie," a familiar voice said between panting breaths, ragged with exertion yet fundamentally calm. "What's this, then?"

Joey snapped back to himself. The wild roaring in his ears shut off. Such was his dread of Gabriel – the realization he was present, with Joey in such a vulnerable state, snapped Joey back to reality as nothing else could.

"Just looking over your girl." Paulie's simian fingers detached from Joey's mouth. The other men let go, too. Backing away from the wall, Joey tripped on his shorts and trousers, still wadded around his ankles, and fell over.

Paulie laughed as Joey flailed, making himself decent as fast as he could. But Paulie's friends weren't laughing. They were blank-faced, staring at Gabriel.

"Paulie," Gabriel said, still between breaths. He'd run a long way. "You used the phrase 'my girl.' Do you not know its meaning?"

"Oi! Are you in love, MacKenna?" Paulie scoffed. "Do you whisper Cooper's name into your pillow as you lie down to sleep every night?"

As Joey got to his feet, Gabriel's eyes slid over his face. "You're bloodied. Right. Who did it?"

Joey wasn't sure which of Paulie's friends had kicked him. Nor was he sure if he was meant to answer. Wentworth's culture felt a great deal like primary school. So Joey fell back on his old schoolboy's oath never to grass, no matter what. "I don't know."

"Fair enough." Whirling, Gabriel came at Paulie in a blur, something small and metallic in his hand. Paulie screamed – high, gut wrenching, primal. As Gabriel released him, Paulie staggered back, a long steel nail protruding from his left eye.

"Pull it out! Pull it out!" Paulie screamed at his friends.

Lips compressed, eyes wide with terror, the braver of the pair grasped the nail and jerked it free. Paulie screamed even louder as a gush of blood and what Joey knew must be aqueous humor shot from the ruptured orb.

"Joey," Gabriel said in his ear.

Joey recoiled. Only with effort did he look at the man who'd protected him.

"Say as little as possible. Admit nothing. I'll see you tonight in commons." Then Gabriel was off, sprinting back to safety.

Soon Joey found himself under intense scrutiny, along with his recently reappeared F-block brethren. They'd abandoned him to warn Gabriel, Joey realized, surprised by his sudden emotional response. Was it twisted, feeling gratitude to one rapist for saving him from another? Feeling warmth for the men who recognized Gabriel's ownership of him and hatred for the men who ignored it?

I'm losing my mind, Joey thought, not for the first time. *Maybe I'm dead. Maybe the train crashed on the journey to Findley. The person I took for Dr. Pfiser was really Satan, and Wentworth is really hell.*

But surely hell would make sense. And Wentworth

made no sense, none at all. Under direct questioning from the lieutenant governor, Joey, Paulie's friends and even Paulie himself repeated the same ludicrous refrain. They had no idea who'd blinded Paulie with a nail – just a mystery man without a face. The lieutenant governor had speculated, threatened, even hinted he might be permitted to birch obstructive witnesses. But beaten by a sea of mute, gormless faces, the lieutenant governor finally gave up. The guards bundled Paulie off to the infirmary to have the empty white shell of his eye removed and the lid sewn over the socket.

That night Joey didn't sleep ten minutes together. He'd felt certain Gabriel would at last demand repayment, and after that brief, terrifying moment with his ass bared to Paulie, Joey didn't think he could withstand it. Which would be better? A deep vertical slash up each wrist? The tremors, the ensuing chill, the disintegration into absolute darkness? Or should he take his chances with that rampant heartbeat, that wild roaring in his ears? To survive in body if not in mind?

Yet Gabriel kept to the bottom bunk. Now he had a torch, won from McCrory, and kept it discreetly under his blanket, reading far into the night. Presently he was re-reading *The Adventure of Huckleberry Finn* and seemed to find it more necessary than sleep.

Sometime around the fourth week, Joey began suffering a new kind of anxiety. It had been a long time, longer than he could remember, since he'd had sufficient quiet and privacy to take care of himself.

Before his arrest, Joey had pleasured himself whenever he needed it, twice a day if necessary, often thinking of his fiancée, Julia. But that was all spoilt now. He wouldn't be permitted to visit Julia face to face until Christmastide, and if she didn't end things at that meeting, he would. He wasn't such a monstrous egotist that he would expect any woman to wait eighteen years for him, then wed him under a cloud of disgrace. Even thinking of Julia, recalling his hands traveling up her skirt, her slender body pressed against his, brought Joey no pleasure. Only shame that he'd let her down, tarred her good name with his own.

There was no way he could see to himself in the cell. Pissing and shitting in the bucket was humiliating enough; leaning over it to masturbate was unthinkable. One morning Joey awakened with a painfully stiff cock. That night when he tried to fall asleep the urge to stroke it, squeeze and pull it, was overwhelming. Joey managed to force his mind elsewhere – mentally reciting the elements of the periodic table was a good distraction. But a bit later he woke up with his hand down his pajama bottoms, bunk springs squeaking and halfway there.

Gabriel, he thought, terrified. With effort Joey relinquished his grip. As quietly as possible he shifted, placing his hands at his sides and willing himself to relax.

"Will you not finish?" a quiet voice asked from the bunk below.

Joey didn't know how to answer.

The bunk springs below gave a low squeak,

signaling a man rising. Then Gabriel was up the steel
ladder, invading Joey's bunk with his long, lean body.
In the mirror-reflected light of the security beacon,
Joey saw Gabriel wore only pajama bottoms, his chest
bare except for a bit of curling dark hair.

"Go on," he murmured. Gabriel was handsome in
the half-light, compactly muscled without an ounce of
fat, that big cock tenting the fabric between his thighs.

Joey shook his head.

"Let me, then." Gently, Gabriel slid Joey's pajamas
down to his knees. A firm grip closed over his cock,
working up and down with the assuredness of an
expert.

Joey didn't dare look at Gabriel. Behind his eyelids,
all he saw was the white-tiled shower floor, pink
water swirling around the drain. So in desperation
Joey thought of Lionel Coates's gardens. After his
natural father finally acknowledged him at age fifteen,
Joey had spent three summers working in those
gardens to earn pocket money. Boxwoods, perennial
shrubberies, apple and pear trees, daisies and
carnations ...

Gabriel's hand was moving faster. Joey's breath
sped up – he couldn't help himself, it felt too good.
Determined, he shifted his thoughts back to the
Coates garden. He'd loved working there, not for
Coates's sake – they were nothing to each other – and
not even for the wages, though his mum needed them
desperately. Joey had simply loved it, never ashamed
to break a sweat or get his hands dirty. There was
truth in the earth, the sunlight. In roots and maggots
and horseshit fertilizer. And great satisfaction in

settling a small, vulnerable plant into the crust of the world, giving it love, tamping it down and watering ... watering ...

Hearing himself groan, Joey pressed his hands to his mouth, thoughts of the Coates garden disappearing. He was coming, the violence of his response proving he was at least as much mere animalistic nerve endings as he was a higher being with an immortal soul.

"Joey," Gabriel said in a husky voice. He kissed the tip of Joey's softening cock. Then Gabriel had himself in hand, working frantically, gritting his teeth until he gasped, spilling a stream of hot fluid onto Joey's belly. The cum had barely ceased before he was atop Joey, pressing their bodies together as his mouth worked against Joey's chest, throat, lips.

"Joey." Gabriel's mouth was beside his ear as Joey, flinching, turned his face away. "Will you not kiss the man who saved you from Paulie?"

Joey tried. Giving in would be so much safer than resisting. But he found he couldn't part his lips or open his eyes. He was frozen, unable to fight, unable to submit.

Gabriel let out a furious exhalation. Rolling off Joey, he clanged down the ladder to his own bunk.

"I – I'm sorry," Joey said, afraid of what retribution the next day might bring.

"Fuck you." The bottom bunk springs gave a vicious squeak as Gabriel flopped toward the wall.

The next day, Joey got the silent treatment from Gabriel. He wasn't even offered any cigarettes, though when he finally struck up the courage to ask, the box was pushed wordlessly toward him. Gabriel put aside his current book and started reading his Bible. According to Lonnie, who noted the change with widened eyes, it signified a very bad mood.

The second night, Joey had no sooner settled himself on the top bunk than Gabriel was up the steel ladder and on the mattress beside him, battery-powered torch in hand. Gabriel dropped it between them so the beam illuminated their faces.

"It's down to this. Kiss me like you mean it – mouth open, using your tongue – for as long as I fancy," Gabriel said. "Or suck my cock and swallow my cum. Your choice."

Joey sat up. He was relieved to find he wasn't trembling. In the torch's muted glow, he saw Gabriel wasn't erect yet, wasn't intimidating.

I can do this, Joey told himself. *At least I'll be in control.*

"Lie back," Joey said, putting all his strength in his voice – the authoritative manner he'd learned in medical school.

Gabriel blinked. For a split second, his disappointment showed through. Then he smiled, stretching out and lacing his fingers together beneath his head. "Grand. But mind you. Don't spit or I'll take it personal."

Servicing Gabriel wasn't difficult. Joey started by curling his fingers around the other man's shaft. It was both familiar and shockingly foreign, sending a ripple of unease through his belly. Once, as a boy, he'd touched a playmate there, permitting his own penis to be examined in turn. But that had been innocent exploration. Holding Gabriel's stiffening cock was strange, frightening, even exhilarating. When Joey used his thumb to stroke it, squeezing slowly, Gabriel sighed, affirming that for the moment, Joey truly was in control.

Joey brought his lips down to the thick, bulbous head. It was surprisingly soft against his tongue, velvety and warm. Taking the huge thing in his mouth, Joey remembered the one and only time he'd received such attention, from a Parisian prostitute called Monique. It was the warmth and wetness that had captivated him – that, and the view of her pink lips sliding up and down.

Imitating the action, Joey looked up. As he expected, Gabriel was watching him. Yes. It was easy, surprisingly easy. If Joey kept a good rhythm and managed not to gag himself, he would do fine. He could use his tongue to vary the action, keep it hot and slick. Maybe he wasn't practiced like Lonnie, but eventually Gabriel would have to—

The other man grunted as if stabbed. A gush of fluid flooded the back of Joey's throat, thick, salty and erotic. Shocked by the stiffness in his balls, the faint clench deeper inside, Joey swallowed reflexively, telling himself he was lucky he didn't vomit. But he didn't feel nauseated. And usually that ripple in his lower belly signaled anything but disgust.

After that first time, Gabriel lasted longer and longer, climbing the ladder every night after lights out. Stretching out on his back, he kept his eyes open until the final moment, watching Joey's mouth work by the torch's soft glow.

"What do you think about while you do it?" Gabriel asked one night in his drowsy, post-orgasm tone.

"Nothing special." Joey kept his pajamas on during each session. When he finished, he curled near Gabriel's feet, knees drawn up to his chin, waiting for the other man to return to his own bed. "Gardening, mostly."

Gabriel made a startled noise. "Are you serious?"

Joey nodded, uncertain how to interpret the other man's look.

"I figured you thought about tits and pussies. Fucking a girl."

Joey felt himself grinning for what felt like the first time in years. "I have a pretty good imagination. But there's no way I could think about a woman with that piece of meat in my mouth."

Grinning back at him, Gabriel sat up. He stretched out a hand to Joey's face, then stopped. "Must you always flinch?"

Joey's grin faded.

"Your smile is lovely. Wish I saw it more often." Sighing, Gabriel climbed back down to his bunk.

F our days later, Joey was removed from the B-block renovation and assigned to Wentworth's vegetable garden. McCrory, the guard who'd delivered the news, had a lit Pall Mall in his hand and a fresh box in his top left pocket. Joey wondered how much of Gabriel's personal stash, maintained by his skill at cards, had gone toward arranging this transfer.

Working the gardens was wonderful. Joey had fresh air, sunlight, the scent of cut grass and crumbled earth beneath his fingernails. When he returned to his cell after that first day, his back ached and his arms were sore, but he couldn't stop smiling. Several times he'd forgotten Joey Cooper's special misery, forgotten the existence of Joey Cooper altogether, and merely assisted the gardener, Mr. Cranston, as directed. Best of all, he would work in gardens Monday through Saturday. Work detail had become a treat.

When Gabriel settled in his bunk, Joey eagerly put his mouth on the other man's cock, intent on making him come harder than ever before. He'd been at it for only a minute or two before Gabriel said, "That must be one hell of a shrub you're thinking about."

Joey stopped, lifting his head and cracking up helplessly. For a long time he and Gabriel could only look at each other. As soon as one managed to quiet, the other started chuckling, beginning the laughter all over again.

"Right," Gabriel said at last. "Let's try something new. Strip. Lie down and let me gaze on you. I'll do the rest."

Unbuttoning his pajama top, Joey cast it away. He wasn't afraid, not really, even as his nipples hardened with the chill. His pajama bottoms and shorts came off with surprising ease. As he stretched out beside Gabriel, the other man placed the torch between them so Joey's full length was illuminated.

"You're beautiful," Gabriel said softly. His hand curled around his cock. "You don't have to watch if you don't want."

Joey closed his eyes, then opened them again. He was stirred, half-erect. He watched for a while as Gabriel's hand worked, eyes open and fixed on Joey's. Then Joey's hand crept down and they were both doing it, eyes locked together, pulling harder as their breath came faster. Joey came first, moaning, and then Gabriel followed with a gasp.

"You didn't go away that time," Gabriel said as Joey panted, dazed.

"No."

Gabriel's fingers touched Joey's cheek. He moved nearer, incrementally closer, as Joey waited, eyes still open. Finally their faces were together. Stroking Joey's hair, Gabriel kissed Joey, first on closed lips, then on the forehead. Joey trembled at the contact, but not with fear. The brush of those long fingers, that hard mouth, was erotic. Then Gabriel released him.

"Best – best get some sleep." Suddenly, Gabriel couldn't look at Joey or get back to his own bunk fast enough. "Cranston will ship you back to unskilled labor if you can't match his pace." With that, he disappeared below, leaving Joey alone in the top bunk, pondering the moment deep into the night.

The next morning, Joey received a letter addressed to him in an unfamiliar hand. It was postmarked London; already opened and read, the envelope had been stamped APPROVED. Joey sat down at the small table to read the letter as Gabriel brushed his teeth at the basin.

Joey—

I wanted to tell you in person. But you won't be permitted your first visitor until December. I wrote the board of governors asking for an exception, but it was denied. So all I have left is to tell you in a letter.

You know I always believed in you. I still do. I have never doubted your innocence. If you were only due to be away for a year, or three years, I could bear it. Not just the loss of your company and my own loneliness, but my shame and isolation, too. I know you'll despise me for telling you this, but when the Crown convicted you, it convicted me, too. Most of the villagers at home wanted nothing to do with me, once they realized I wouldn't gossip about you. So I moved to London to stay with my cousin Dora. I don't expect I shall ever go home again. I am starting a new life in the city and for it to succeed, it must be new in every way.

Joey, please understand, I don't expect you to forgive me. It must seem as though the entire world has turned against you, through no fault of your own, and now me, too. What I have chosen is selfish, and wrong, and I've chosen it all the same. I want to live while I'm young enough to have the things I once dreamt of – a husband, children, and a good name.

Julia

Joey stared at the letter. It was all in Julia's handwriting, except for the signature, which was bold and slanted. Studying the smudge on the words "young" and "name," Joey suspected Julia had wept so much while making her confession, she'd been unable to continue. So cousin Dora had signed the letter, written directions on the envelope and posted it.

He was proud of Julia, happy for her. Her choice was what he'd wanted, echoing the very arguments he'd used during those black days after he was convicted and awaiting sentencing. Even if they'd been wed, Joey would have urged Julia to divorce him. The very idea of a twenty-three-year-old woman, bright and pretty and vivacious, waiting eighteen years for her fiancé to emerge from prison, middle-aged and no doubt broken, was obscene. What would Joey have to offer her by then? Disgraced as a physician and fit for nothing but manual labor, assuming he could even get it ...

Gabriel slipped the letter out of Joey's fingers and pressed a clean handkerchief in its place. "Right. To your bunk."

Wiping his eyes, Joey struggled to control of

himself. "It's not – it's not the letter," Joey said, or tried to say, throat closing as Gabriel helped him up. "It's just – just—"

"In your bunk," Gabriel repeated. "I'll report you as sick to the duty guard. He'll check on you once an hour, ask if you need the infirmary. Otherwise you'll be left in peace."

Joey felt fresh grief well up, not for the loss of Julia, whom he couldn't see, couldn't talk to, couldn't touch, but for himself – the last remnant of his old life, lost forever. Still in his uniform and heavy standard-issue shoes, Joey lay atop the rough gray blanket, turned his face to the wall and sobbed until no more tears would come.

When Gabriel returned after work detail, Joey was sitting at the table again, smoking a cigarette. Julia's letter was tucked in his left breast pocket.

"Lonnie said you were a carpenter before." Joey nodded at the faint layer of sawdust on Gabriel's uniform.

"Still am." Gabriel brushed at his trouser legs. "The governor and the administrators use me shamelessly, right under the eyes of God, a master carpenter's free labor. And they know I won't botch it up just to spite them, 'cause I take too much infernal pride in my work. Once the world learns the source of your pride, it owns you."

"I would say, the source of your shame."

"Ah. Well. That, too." Pulling out the little table's other chair, Gabriel turned it around and straddled it. An unlit Pall Mall appeared in his hand as if by magic. "Joey. Whatever news the letter brought. I'm damned sorry for it."

Joey stared into Gabriel's hazel eyes. The rectangular face, the high cheekbones, the firm chin and creased forehead – he was utterly masculine, hard as granite except for those eyes. Like the eyes of a great predator, a cheetah or lion, Gabriel's eyes could be soulful, hypnotic, beautiful.

Joey laughed. The sound was nothing like usual. Was the old Joey Cooper gone for good? Had his earlier outpouring of grief been the death knell?

Gabriel seemed unoffended by the laughter. "I know, 'tis useless to go round saying sorry for things we'd naught to do with, nor any power to heal. But—" He broke off, transparently startled when Joey struck a match and lit his cigarette for him. "Why. Thank you."

"I wasn't laughing because you said sorry about the letter. That was decent. Polite." Taking a drag off his cigarette, Joey blew smoke out his nostrils. "I was laughing because you had the bollocks to say sorry for a letter you never read and not for what you did to me in the showers."

Gabriel stared back silently for so long, Joey began to think the other man wouldn't respond in words. He braced himself for Gabriel to leap to his feet, overturn the table, curse and rage. But Joey didn't shrink away. Part of him welcomed it.

At last Gabriel put the Pall Mall to his lips and inhaled. "If could take it back, I would."

Pointing with his own cigarette, Joey leaned across the table, stabbing the lit end mere centimeters from the tip of Gabriel's nose. "Not an apology."

"You wouldn't accept it."

"You don't get to say what I'll do with it!" Joey cried, on his feet all in one motion. "Last night you – I – we almost—"

Cigarette held between taut lips, Gabriel was also on his feet, catching Joey's arms and overpowering him with ease. "Quiet," he said, forcing Joey back into his chair. "Say your peace but say it low, unless you want us both birched for fighting."

"Everyone who should have stood by me turned away," Joey said fiercely, trembling all over. "I wanted Julia to join them, I asked for it, I expected it. The only thing left that doesn't make sense is you." Joey glared up into Gabriel's face. "I hate you. I don't want your protection. Let them kill me!" Flinging down the half-smoked cigarette, Joey crushed it under his heel, wishing everything could be stamped out so easily.

"Joey—"

"No more! I'm done with you. Let them kill me or kill me yourself," Joey cried, throwing himself back on the bunk and covering his face. For a long time there was silence. Then Joey heard Gabriel's footfalls departing as the other man headed for the cafeteria, and supper.

When Joey woke up, the cell was locked down and the overhead lights were snuffed. With effort, he managed to read his wristwatch in the mirror-reflected light: eleven thirty. Gabriel was probably still awake below, immersed in a novel. It didn't matter. Joey's bladder was too full for him to remain in the bunk much longer.

He climbed down the steel ladder as quietly as his prison-issue shoes allowed. Slipping them off, Joey made it within half a meter of the bucket when Gabriel spoke.

"Careful now. Don't kick it over. I took a shit in there the size of the Albert Hall."

Joey heard himself chuckle. This time the sound wasn't the mirthless noise of a stranger. When he finished with the bucket he sighed, muscles relaxing, and sat down at the little table.

"If the guards catch you sitting there after lights out, they'll order you back to your bunk."

"I've spent too much time there already."

Gabriel threw his long legs over the side of his bunk. Feeling around for his pajama bottoms, he pulled them on and sat down across from Joey bare-chested. "Fancy a smoke?"

"God, yes."

Gabriel lit two Pall Malls and passed one over. Joey took a grateful drag.

"You never asked what I'm in for," Gabriel said

after they'd smoked in silence for a while. "Guess someone told you."

"They said the charge was originally double murder. Your father ...?"

Gabriel nodded. "If you kill your father, they call it patricide. Your mother? Matricide. Do them both in one night, send your parents side by side into the next world, and there's no word grand enough for it. Which is funny," Gabriel said, "because in the history of the whole human race, I can't be the only sorry bastard who's done it."

Joey brought his cigarette to his lips again. Gabriel waited a moment, then reached across the table and poked Joey lightly in the shoulder. "This is where you ask me why I did it."

"Why did you do it?"

"I was the eldest MacKenna." Gabriel's gaze slid away from Joey's. "My sister Maureen was ten years younger. I loved all my family, you know how that goes, but I loved Maureen best. She was my plaything, my own little girl. Used to nurse her with a bottle and rock her on my knee. One day in summertime she came to me crying. Pregnant. I said, tell me his name. He'll marry you or go to his grave and there's an end to it. But she wouldn't say. First time Maureen ever refused me when I was in a state. I bellowed and threatened, but all she did was cry. I thought the bastard was married." Gabriel gave a humorless laugh. "Anyway. Next week she tells me it's all over, she got rid of it. I knew a mad old bat down the lane did abortions. But I never thought Maureen would go for one, come hell or high water. And she hadn't. She'd been made to do it. Being with child frightened my little sister but she wanted the baby, wanted someone of her own to love. Being forced to let that old woman rake into her ..." Gabriel took a deep drag off his Pall Mall. "The guilt tore Maureen to bits. I grabbed her and shook her until she gave up the name of the man responsible."

"Your father."

"Oh, yes. Keeping it all in the family, don't you know?" Gabriel took another pull off his cigarette. "And me such a damned fool, I never guessed. All us kids were scared shitless of the old man, he'd cuff us soon as look at us, but I never knew he poked his fingers up the lasses' skirts. And Mum knew. God help us, she knew. When Maureen confessed he'd gone farthest with her, taking her to bed, I ... well. You know how they say an angry man sees red?" Gabriel's mouth stretched, but his eyes were blank. "'Tis true. The world went crimson. Maybe it was the devil coming over me, I don't know. I smoked and paced the back garden while Mum cooked supper. The second Da came home, the second he entered the kitchen through the back door, I was on him. Don't remember what I said. Don't remember how it felt. But I broke Da's neck with my bare hands."

Joey tried to imagine such a thing. But Lionel Gates had never truly been a father to him. The adoration, the fear, the father-son rivalry – it was all foreign to Joey. Even when Coates had been moved at the sight of his pretty bastard boy, even when he was charmed by Joey's popularity within the village, Coates had done no more than hire Joey to work in his gardens.

Every other advantage Joey had enjoyed, including his scholarship to Oxford, was earned through personal merit alone.

"Tell me everything," Joey said when Gabriel didn't continue. "I can guess. But tell me."

Gabriel smiled again. This time it touched his eyes, crinkling the skin around them, and something in Joey's frozen midsection turned over. The man was handsome. Not just physically, not just in face and form. Within those eyes.

"Two things run in my family on my mum's side," Gabriel continued. "Ginger hair and madness. I don't have the ginger hair. I'm the only MacKenna of my generation who doesn't. Neither did my Aunt Sally, but she had the madness, don't you know. Always jabbering to the saints, which every Irish woman does, but in her case they jabbered back a little too much. As for my mum – she had the ginger hair *and* the madness. She was mad for my da. He was meat and drink to her – the sun and moon in one suitcase, if you mark me. Loved Da more than me and all the other kids put together. When I took Da by the throat, she came at me with a cast-iron skillet. Don't remember taking it from her, or knocking her down. But it must have been a hell of a blow because," he sighed, blowing out smoke, "she died a few hours after they arrested me."

"Did you flee?" Joey wondered what he would have done in Gabriel's place. He couldn't imagine lifting a finger to his mum. But she was gentle, easy and utterly his. It wasn't true that he'd lost every remnant of his former life. His mum would wait faithfully for his release as long as her health held out.

"Flee?" Gabriel blinked at Joey as if returning from someplace far away.

"Do a runner? Hide?"

"No. Never occurred to me. Next thing I remember, I was sitting at the kitchen table. My little brother Joseph came in – twenty years old if he was a day but never missed a meal at home – and called the constable. At the trial he gave evidence against me." Gabriel shrugged. "'Twas the right thing to do. The only thing.

"The Met charged me with double murder. But Maureen offered to testify for me. Told the whole story, every bit of it, though she knew she'd never be able to hold up her head in the old neighborhood again. The abortionist was arrested. Maureen, too. Forced to submit to a medical exam." Gabriel sighed again. "You know I meant to protect her. But all I did was shame her, shame myself and destroy our family. If I'd asked her, she would have rather pretended it never happened. Instead she was named in the papers, just like me. That's how Rebecca Eisenberg got involved."

"Rebecca Eisenberg?" Joey didn't recognize the name.

"Social reformer. Prison reformer. Women's rights reformer," Gabriel added with both eyebrows raised, as if daring Joey to mock her. "Rebecca found a solicitor and got Maureen off straightaway. She even tried to help the mad old bat who did the abortion, but that was a lost cause. There were too many other complaints, too many women coming forward, maimed for life. Then Rebecca took my case, entirely on Maureen's word, before ever meeting me. You know the type? Doesn't believe any man should hang, no matter what he's done. Has a million and one arguments – Jesus, Buddha, Paddy down t'pub, any authority you can think of. And she engaged a barrister who defended me on the grounds of 'irresistible impulse.'"

"I've heard of that," Joey said. "It doesn't mean a man is insane. It means he was so provoked, so inflamed, he couldn't help himself. So he would have committed the exact same crime even if a policeman had been standing at his elbow."

"Well done." Gabriel lit a new Pall Mall off the dog-end of the old. Joey studied Gabriel through the wreath of smoke, tempted to reach across the table and touch the other man's hand.

Not because what he did to me doesn't matter. Even in his lowest moments, Joey didn't value himself so little. But because in this place where he'd lost so much, where nearly every comfort had been taken away, he alone had the power to forgive Gabriel. And with the realization of his power came the sweet, painful temptation to use it.

"So. I was spared from the noose, as you see," Gabriel continued dryly. "I'd been prepared to die. Confess, be shriven, and go. Suddenly I was looking at the rest of my life as a prisoner without hope of parole. I was so angry I could have strangled Rebecca," he added, grinning. "She came to see me as soon as permitted. I walked into the visiting room ready to tell her just what I thought of her – her and all the do-gooders who stuck me here for eternity, or near as makes no difference, to think on what I'd done. Then I saw her."

Joey couldn't read Gabriel's expression. "You mean – she was pretty?"

"Thirty-five or forty. A spinster. Dressed like a blind man picked her clothes. Hatchet face and big brown cow eyes," Gabriel smiled fondly. "Do you know, Rebecca earned a law degree? Top marks, but couldn't find anywhere to practice, being a woman. Earned a doctorate in sociology, too, what do you think of that? And there I was, with my primary school education, feeling superior to her because she was homely. But ignorance pushed me to do the right thing. I swallowed my bile and thanked her humbly. And she said saving a man from a meaningless death was its own reward."

"Do you still hear from her?"

"Sure and I do." Gabriel winked as if discussing an old girlfriend. "We correspond, don't you know? Discuss books and what not. She visits me twice a year. Closest thing to a wife I'll ever have."

"What happened to Maureen?"

"Took the veil. Joined the Benedictines as Sister Mary Michael. Says she's found true peace with God. Writes me every Christmas and Easter to say she loves me and prays for my soul." Gabriel stopped, looking across the table to meet Joey's gaze. He opened his mouth to say more, then closed it, plainly unable to get the words out.

"Gabe," Joey put his hand on the other man's. "Last night felt good. Not just getting off. After. Why did you pull away?"

Gabriel's eyes dropped. Shifting the Pall Mall to his mouth, he placed his other hand atop Joey's, his two hands enclosing Joey's slightly smaller one. "Forgive me."

Torchlight flashed into the cell. Buckland, who'd pulled night duty for the month, pretended not to notice as they hastily pulled apart.

"For Chrissake, MacKenna, Cooper, what're you doing? Holding a séance? Trying to make contact with a dead witness since all the live ones say you're guilty?"

Joey, shaken by the interruption, didn't know what to say, but Gabriel chuckled. Maintaining close relations with guards like McCrory and Buckland served him well.

"Just woke up to find Cooper sick over the bucket. Fancy a visit to the infirmary yet?" Gabriel turned to Joey.

"No. I'm better. Back to meals and work detail tomorrow, I promise."

"Good man." Approaching the bars, Buckland lowered his voice. "MacKenna. Cranston showed me the restoration you did on his sideboard. Bang-up job."

"Re-hung the doors. Carved in some flourishes. Sanded it down and slapped on a coat of varnish." Gabriel shrugged with perfectly false modesty.

"Well, you know my Bettie's expecting," Buckland said. "The cradle her mum gave us is wooden, older than Queen Victoria and twice as ugly. If I brought it round, could you fix it up? Not necessarily during common time. I might be able to shift your work detail."

"Of course."

Buckland grinned. "What'll it cost?"

Gabriel held up his cigarette. "You know."

"Doesn't anyone sleep in this joint?" a man called from further down F-block, prompting Buckland to move along at last.

"You restored furniture for Cranston? Is that how you got me transferred to the gardens?" Joey asked.

"Didn't have much choice. Cranston doesn't gamble, doesn't smoke and doesn't fancy my pretty face." Gabriel rose. "Best get back to our bunks."

Slowly, reluctantly, Joey changed into his pajamas and climbed into the top bunk. Part of him was frustrated that Buckland had interrupted them; part of him was relieved. The moment had been taken from them before he could decide how to respond.

Julia's letter was gone from his mind. Joey fell asleep thinking of Gabriel's hands enclosing his, and all the ways he might have answered.

Next evening, Joey plowed through his supper, rambling about his ideas to improve the vegetable garden's output. Gabriel only sat and smoked, tray of food untouched. Even his cigarette seemed to bring him little pleasure.

"What is it?" Joey asked.

"Nothing. My dinner went down bad, is all. Had a bellyache ever since."

"There's bicarbonate in the infirmary."

Gabriel held up his left hand with its missing little finger. "I'd prefer to keep all the rest of my parts, thank you."

Joey, who'd heard the story three times from Lonnie, understood Gabriel's reluctance to put himself back at Dr. Royal's mercy. But when Gabriel was no better the next morning, and still worse by the third evening, Joey said, "You can't go on this way. Your fever must be pushing a hundred. You could die if you aren't looked after."

"No man ever died from a bad sandwich."

"Sure they have. Botulism. Besides, it could be something else. Is all the pain on your right side?"

Gabriel nodded, flinching away when Joey tried to touch him there. He was pale, forehead damp with sweat.

Joey frowned. "Gabe, it could be your appendix."

"Meaning what?"

Joey tried to think how to say it. "You might need an operation."

Gabriel's eyes went wide. "Fuck no. I won't be put under. Won't be cut open in my sleep. I'll die first."

Getting to his feet, Joey paced restlessly. His own supper weighed heavily on his stomach. The more he thought about Gabriel's symptoms, the more he worried. A boy in Joey's home village had died of a burst appendix. Timely intervention was essential; once the infection spread through the gut, death was almost assured.

"Hey! Buckland! Someone!" Joey called, pounding on the bars with a library book. "I need help! I'm sick!"

"Goddamn it," Gabriel snarled, trying to sit up and failing. "You think it was bad in the showers? I'll hurt you worse, I'll fucking kill you, don't you grass on me, Joey, don't you tell them—"

Buckland turned up, crumbs from his supper decorating his tie. The moment he saw Gabriel, his expression changed from curiosity to genuine concern. "Cooper? Are you and MacKenna both sick this time?"

Joey nodded. "Think it's ptomaine. I can't stop retching. And Gabe can't even get out of bed."

"I'm grand, goddamn it," Gabriel said through his teeth.

"Help me get him up," Buckland said to Joey, entering the cell with a wary eye on Gabriel.

They advanced on Gabriel together. Dodging Gabriel's clumsy punch, Joey caught the other man's arm and twisted it behind his back. Gabriel gasped, eyes bright with tears. Joey knew it wasn't just the wrestling hold. Gabriel was in so much pain, even he couldn't hide it.

"Do as I say or I'll break your arm and drag you to the infirmary," Joey whispered in Gabriel's ear. "For once in your life, do the smart thing, not the brave thing."

Doubled over, Gabriel allowed Joey and Buckland to steer him out of F-block and down two long halls to the infirmary. The small pharmacopeia and surgery was deserted. In the doctors' private quarters, Dr.

Royal was taking his dinner, complete with silver cutlery and sherry. Cursing at the interruption, Dr. Royal started to take Buckland to task for the interruption, then caught sight of Gabriel. Tossing aside his linen napkin, Dr. Royal stood up. The curl to his lips and sudden gleam in his eyes made Joey want to punch him. Instead he rushed to the doctor, clutching his belly.

"I'm bad off, doc! Me first!"

"All in good time," Dr. Royal said, barely sparing Joey a glance. "MacKenna appears in more urgent need."

As Dr. Royal pushed past him, Joey jabbed his fingers down his throat. Whirling, he caught Dr. Royal by the shoulder as his entire supper came up. The reeking, half-digested mess sprayed all over the doctor's white coat, trousers and shoes.

"Oh, Christ! Ben! I need you in here!" Dr. Royal bellowed.

Dr. Harper appeared as Dr. Royal tore off his soiled white coat and threw it at Joey. He stalked off, muttering, to change his clothes as Dr. Harper approached the inmates. Gabriel, now unable to stand even with Buckland's help, sunk to the floor. Dr. Harper hurried to his side.

"How long has he been like this?" Dr. Harper asked Joey.

"Three days. It's appendicitis." Joey didn't back down from the other physician's sharp glance. "I'm sure of it."

"I see. Taught you about appendicitis at Oxford, did they?" Dr. Harper performed a quick exam, ignoring

Gabriel's moans of protest. "Fine diagnosis, Dr. Cooper. But we don't have the facilities to deal with appendicitis. He'll need to go to hospital. Buckland! Phone Gerber. Have him pull the car around. It'll be quicker to take MacKenna direct than to wait on an ambulance."

"No," Gabriel whispered, staring up at Joey, eyes pleading.

"Can I go with him?" Joey asked Dr. Harper.

The other doctor blinked in astonishment. "Of course not."

Joey eased down beside Gabriel. As Dr. Harper went to the window, waiting for the car's headlights to appear, Joey slid an arm around Gabriel's shoulders. The other man was trembling.

"It's all right," Joey said. "You'll be in a real hospital far from Dr. Royal. No one will hurt you there."

"I told you. I hate doctors. My brother Robbie's crippled because—" Gabriel broke off as another spasm of pain shook him. "I'm afraid, Joey."

"I know. But I've gone with you as far as I can. And I'll be waiting for you, I promise."

"Here's Gerber with the car," Dr. Harper announced, turning back to Joey and Gabriel, only to glance quickly away again. Surely Dr. Harper was accustomed to such moments - prisoners embracing like brothers or lovers - but he looked embarrassed nonetheless.

"Remember," Joey said, kissing Gabriel gently on the lips, "I'll be waiting for you."

Gabriel returned to Wentworth four days later. He was walked back to his cell by McCrory and greeted with cheers, lighthearted insults and even a few unlit cigarettes that McCrory dutifully scooped up and delivered. Joey wasn't there – it was midafternoon, he was still on work detail – so Gabriel eased into the bottom bunk to wait. He could have opted for transfer directly to Wentworth's infirmary, where he would have been allowed narcotics for his postoperative pain, but vehemently refused. Funny – Gabriel had been outside Wentworth for the first time in nearly six years and all he'd wanted was to get inside again. For better or worse, F-block was his home now.

The sisters at St. George's Hospital had been kind. During the worst of his pain, just before surgery and the day following, the ward sister had insisted Gabriel's leg and wrist shackles be removed. And he'd called out for Joey so often, the sister had done a bit of digging, discovered the whereabouts of Gabriel's younger brother Joseph, and prevailed upon him to come and visit.

The meeting had begun badly and turned worse. Fr. Joseph MacKenna hadn't seen or spoken to Gabriel since giving evidence against him at the trial. He'd testified to finding Gabriel sitting blank-faced at the kitchen table, their father dead on the floor, their mother lying unresponsive atop her husband. When asked if his elder brother was often vicious or cruel, Joseph had replied that all men outside the Lord's influence were sinful. His characterization of Gabriel as a lustful, worldly man had seriously harmed Gabriel's defense. But Gabriel hadn't borne Joseph any ill will. Of all Gabriel's little brothers and sisters, Joseph alone had seen Da dead with a purple face and Mum with a dent in her skull. It wasn't something any son was likely to forgive.

"They tell me you were calling for me," Joseph had begun, pursing his lips and twisting his soft pale hands together. He'd grown plump since putting on the dog collar. Like Maureen, Joseph had entered the Body of Christ soon after the murders, but in Joseph's case, the vows were already planned. And Joseph, unlike Maureen, had never sent Gabriel any letters offering personal forgiveness or prayers for his soul.

"I wasn't surprised," Joseph continued. "A brush with death makes even the proudest man crave forgiveness."

"I wasn't calling for you. I was calling for Joey. The sisters were confused."

"I see," Joseph said, though he clearly didn't. Perhaps he believed his elevation to the priesthood required him to feign special intellectual powers. "And who is Joey?"

"My cellmate."

Joseph looked uncomfortable. "Gabriel. I know it must be hell for you in there. But after what you did, you had it coming. I would hope you've used your incarceration to study. Meditate. Give your heart to Christ. Not get up to anything ... unnatural."

Gabriel studied Joseph, perceiving him suddenly as an adult stranger, not the little brother who'd loved baking and paper dolls and watching afternoon matinees with his sisters.

"Unnatural, is it?" Gabriel said at last. "I'll wager you know as much about it as I do. Climbed on your share of boys in seminary, did you?"

Joseph's pale face went even paler. "You – you monster."

Gabriel had laughed so hard, his incision site throbbed for hours. "At least I can admit I'm fucking a man," he'd called as his brother scurried away, black dress flapping. "Come back when you can!"

Gabriel was still chuckling over the memory when Joey arrived. The younger man strolled up to the lower bunk, hands in his pockets and smiling to shame the sun, as Gabriel's grandmother used to say. The sight was as welcome as Gabriel's first post-op Pall Mall.

"You're thinner," Joey said.

"They cut out part of me and threw it away. Takes a man's appetite."

"If I fetch a tray in here, will you eat?"

"Perhaps if you feed me." Gabriel beckoned. Joey came closer, squatting beside the lower bunk with a hand on the ladder to steady himself.

"Joey. Before the ambulance took me – I'm not proud of how I acted. Came over as a bit of a coward, didn't I?"

Joey traced the line of Gabriel's face from temple to jaw, running fingers over the stiff beard growth. "I've missed you."

Gabriel's stomach dropped. Something about the surgery had heightened his emotions, difficult to manage even in the best of times. His anger frightened him because he was helpless against it. Now he was helpless against this feeling, too. "Come in here with me."

Gently, Joey slid into the bunk, putting his back to the wall so their bodies touched only on Gabriel's left side. "Still in pain?"

"God, yes. I don't care."

Joey moved close to Gabriel, trying not to lean against him too much. Still, the sutures at Gabriel's incision site pulled taut. Fresh sweat beaded his forehead. But he slid his arm around Joey and held him tight.

"You saved my life." Gabriel rested his forehead against Joey's, keeping their flesh together 'til he was able to continue. "Protected me from my own fool self. Name your price. I'll keep you safe. But if you want all the rest to end, just say so."

Raising himself on one elbow, Joey contemplated Gabriel silently. Then his mouth closed over Gabriel's. Gabriel let himself be kissed, savoring the warmth and wetness, better than any narcotic. Even as his wound stabbed and burned, Gabriel kept kissing Joey hungrily until the other man pulled away.

"I'm hurting you. You need to lie quietly. Rest for a while."

"I'm fine," Gabriel groaned.

"Oh, yes, I can see that." Joey used his sleeve to mop away the perspiration standing out on Gabriel's face. Pushing back a lock of damp hair, Joey kissed

Gabriel's forehead. "Don't worry. The price is set. As soon as you're strong enough, I'll expect payment."

Over the following days Gabriel healed rapidly. Joey attributed this to rest and regular meals; Gabriel attributed it to unrestricted cigarettes and Joey in his bunk each night. Of course, some care had to be taken. Not every guard was like Buckland, indifferent to catching two inmates beneath one blanket. If seen and put on report, both Gabriel and Joey would get the lash. But Gabriel was popular and Joey had also started to make friends among the guards. As long as they weren't blatant about their activities after lights out, they could continue without fear of reprisal.

Every night after reconfinement, after the overheads went dark and the guards' first walk-throughs were done, Joey stuffed two pillows beneath his blanket to simulate a sleeping figure. Decoy in place, he climbed into Gabriel's bunk, remaining there for a few hours each night. Curling against Gabriel's left side, Joey would rest his head against the other man's chest. They talked softly in the darkness, pausing now and then to kiss. For Gabriel that was the best part, better even than holding Joey close – kissing him over and over until their lips were slick and sore. One night Gabriel was so intent on the feel of Joey's tongue against his, the warmth of the other man in his arms, he rolled on top of Joey and kept on kissing him until he realized his side barely ached at all. The tightness in his lower belly, the throbbing need in his cock, outweighed any soreness in his healing wound.

"Name your price," Gabriel whispered, biting the softness of Joey's throat and tugging the skin between his teeth.

"It's something we've never tried." Sliding his lips along Gabriel's bare chest, Joey caught a nipple between his lips and twisted until Gabriel gave a stifled moan. "Sure you're up to it?"

"Oh, I'm up." Gabriel pressed Joey's hand against his cock. "Is the torch in your bunk?"

"It is." Extricating himself with a kiss, Joey climbed up the steel ladder, peeled up his mattress and felt beneath it. Before Gabriel could work out why the torch would be stashed there, Joey was back down again, already stripped to his shorts. He tossed the lighted torch onto Gabriel's bunk and wriggled beneath Gabriel again, soon nude and hard as rock.

"If you mean for me to suck you," Gabriel said, unable to look away from that lovely cock and almost trembling with readiness, "you're the first man to ask since Carl Werth. But I promise not to use all my teeth."

Joey shook his head, smiling the mischievous, self-possessed smile that made secret parts of Gabriel run wild. "Not yet." Joey revealed what he held in his right hand, a steel tube Gabriel at first mistook for toothpaste or Brylcreem. "Lonnie stole this from the infirmary."

"Stole it? What did you promise him in return?"

"A kiss."

Gabriel frowned.

"From you."

"Oh. Sure and I can manage that, I suppose." Unscrewing the cap, Gabriel squeezed a bit of clear jelly onto his fingers and understood. Covering Joey's body with his own, Gabriel kissed his lips. "But you said – something we haven't tried ..."

"We haven't." Reaching up, Joey cupped Gabriel's cheek. "What happened before was one stranger attacking another. What happens now is between you and me."

"Joey." Gabriel kissed the other man's earlobe, his jawline, the hollow of his throat. "I can't hurt you again. I'll kill myself first."

"Then go slow. And stop if I tell you." Joey rubbed the cool, light jelly up and down Gabriel's cock. Then he spread it between his own legs, working so slowly and thoroughly, Gabriel was transfixed. Lifting himself, Joey took hold of Gabriel and pressed the head of his cock inside as much as he could bear.

"Does it hurt?"

"Oh. Give ... give me a moment ..." Joey's eyes locked with Gabriel's, bright with dawning pleasure as well as pain. "Right." He took a deep breath, smiling again. "More, Gabe. More."

Biting his lower lip, Gabriel pushed in. It was easier, much easier than he remembered, partly because of the lubricant, partly because Joey wasn't fighting with all his strength to keep him out. Still Joey grunted as Gabriel slid inside. Heart pounding wildly, Gabriel stopped. Two needs tore at him – desperation to continue and an overriding desire to protect Joey from everything, even himself.

"More," Joey whispered, lifting himself and wrapping his legs around Gabriel's waist.

Closing his eyes, Gabriel pushed forward, groaning at the hot, tight grasp. Then he was inside completely, buried to his balls and rocking gently. Even if Joey couldn't tolerate firmer strokes, this was perfect. Heaven. The most exquisite pleasure of Gabriel's life ...

Joey made a noise, high and agonized.

"Do you want me out?"

"No," Joey gasped. "Faster. Much faster."

Gabriel's hips began to rock. At first he held Joey close, pressing against the whole of his body, skin to skin, a sheen of sweat between them. Then Gabriel shifted, straightening, and Joey's moan was a revelation.

"Like that? There?" Gabriel whispered.

"There." Joey's eyes were open but unfocused. "There ... there ... *oh* ..."

Straightening his back, Gabriel kept at the correct angle, thrusting as hard as he could. Soon his wound was hurting again, hurting like hell, but Joey was trembling, back arched with pleasure, and Gabriel couldn't leave him unfulfilled. He kept on until Joey went rigid, freezing as if in agony. And when Joey clenched tight inside, Gabriel cried out at the top of his lungs.

"Joey – oh, Christ – Joey –" Then Gabriel was coming too, cum gushing like blood from a puncture wound. Falling into the other man's arms, Gabriel buried his face in Joey's ginger-brown hair.

"I love you," he whispered.

Joey, dazed, looked blissfully up at Gabriel as hoots and scattered applause broke out up and down F-block.

"Glad you can still get it up, MacKenna!" someone shouted. "Now can the rest of us get some goddamn sleep?"

After that night – Gabriel's outcry and the cell block rowdiness that followed – one of Wentworth's more stringent guards cottoned on, taking it upon himself to personally police Gabriel and Joey. Each night Victor Hess walked past their cell at different times, examining their bunks with his torch and listening around corners. Buckland refused to take part in the crusade. But to Joey's surprise, McCrory joined in.

"I thought he was your friend," Joey said to Gabriel over breakfast one morning. Twice now they'd nearly been caught, forcing each man to keep to his own bunk after lights out.

"So did I. But he's been a wee bit cold ever since I managed to get the two of us in the same cell." Gabriel shrugged, scraping up the last of his oatmeal and casting a stern glance at Lonnie. Reluctantly, the pretty blond took up his own spoon, though he seemed disinclined to use it. Lonnie had spent the last two weeks in close company with Gordon Lusk, D-block's resident demon. Since then he'd begun trying out new airs and even a bit of verbal defiance. But this didn't extend to Gabriel, so while the other man's eye was upon him, Lonnie made a show of eating up.

For weeks it went on, the surprise inspections, waking to an unlocked cell and light shining in the face. Hess lost interest by midsummer. Moving to G-block, he caught three pairs in the act and made certain all got the lash. But McCrory kept up his new vigilance. During the day he interacted as usual with Gabriel – joking, gambling, trading smokes for favors. But at night McCrory went out of his way to patrol F-block, passing through at different times while trying to catch Gabriel and Joey in the act.

"You're sure about this?" Joey asked when Gabriel steered him into the prison library's stacks, Fiction A-Br.

"Three lookouts. Safe as houses." Gabriel pressed Joey against a bookshelf, arms encircling him as he kissed Joey's ear, his cheek, his neck. "God, I've missed this."

Joey chuckled. They'd met in the garden shed just three days ago, managing a no-holds-barred session while Mr. Cranston was off purchasing a new tiller.

"You do have your needs." Joey lifted himself so their cocks rubbed together through the thin barrier of their prison uniforms. "I'm still sore from last time."

"Should I kiss it for you?"

"Mmmm ..." Just the teasing mention sent fresh

heat into Joey's cheeks. Once Gabriel had done that, parting Joey's legs and stabbing up and up with his tongue until Joey came, half from delight and half from shame. There was no part of Joey that Gabriel didn't want to see, touch, kiss. And each time they made love, Joey surrendered a little more, enjoying the sacrifice even if it left him secret places only inside. And Joey could feel Gabriel pressing on those inner doors, too. Not physically, but with words, glances ... the occasional Gaelic endearment after he thought Joey had fallen asleep ...

Gabriel's hands slid under Joey's shirt, beginning their slow exploration. Gabriel's fingers were long and callused, their roughness sending shivers of pleasure along Joey's flesh. Up his waist they traveled, exploring his chest, digging into his shoulders, stroking his biceps and triceps. Then Gabriel was kissing Joey's mouth again. One hand tangled in his hair while the other stroked Joey's flat belly, teasing the curling hair just below it but never delving down.

"Well?" Gabriel prompted at last. "You said you were sore. A kiss to make it better?"

Lifting himself again, Joey pressed Gabriel's hand against the firmness of his crotch. "This is what needs kissing."

Making a low, pleased rumble in his throat, Gabriel knelt before him. Unbuttoning Joey's fly, he drew him out, fastening his lips on the head of Joey's cock. At first he focused only on the head, tracing its shape with his tongue, exciting it with the rasp of his teeth. Then Gabriel's hands squeezed Joey's ass, pressing Joey entirely in his mouth as he sucked the root. At first Joey watched, fascinated by Gabriel, so handsome, so masculine, eyes shut tight as if he enjoyed the action at least as much as Joey did. Then the rising pressure turned unbearable. Digging his fingers into Gabriel's hair, Joey held the other man steady as he began to thrust. At first Joey was only controlling the motion, setting his own pace. But as climax neared, Joey slammed into Gabriel's mouth with greater and greater need, using him mercilessly until he unloaded with torturous, perfect spasms.

"I – I'm sorry," Joey muttered as he came back to himself. Kneeling beside Gabriel, he was surprised to find the other man smiling. Gabriel's hair was tousled from Joey's grip and his eyes had a slightly unfocused look, as if he, too, had reached his destination.

"Not another man in Wentworth would get so rough with me," Gabriel panted. "Never been fucked that way, not in the whole of my life."

Joey felt a slow grin dawning. He enjoyed the effect he had on Gabriel. Enjoyed seeing the other man grow softer – his gaze, the set of his mouth, the timbre of his voice. "Did you ...?"

"Oh, aye. But leaving a stain on the carpet is an invitation for trouble." Gabriel showed Joey the wadded handkerchief in his right hand. "And I'll not risk splattering books, not even the bad ones."

More than an hour of common time remained, but Gabriel wasn't interested in any of the card games in progress, so they walked back to their unlocked cell. Joey took a pen and a sheet of writing paper to his bunk, determined to progress beyond the salutation *Dear Julia.*

Since first reading Julia's letter, Joey had revisited it several times, each time with a greater realization of what it must have cost her to write it. Julia valued loyalty above all other qualities, with the exception of honesty. To be caught between those two traits – to want freedom, want it desperately, while hating herself for it, must have been agony. Joey thought if he could find the correct words – not sanctimonious, not overly cool, not uncomfortably warm – he might be able to help. To give her permission, so to speak, and lessen her guilt when she thought of him behind bars at Wentworth. After that first terrible rush of anguish and self-pity, Joey had been genuinely glad of Julia's decision. He just didn't know how to tell her in a way that wouldn't injure her all over again.

Gabriel sat down at the small table with a book and a smoke. He wasn't at either for more than a minute before McCrory and Buckland appeared.

"MacKenna." Buckland made a show of rapping on the bars, not entering until Gabriel waved him inside. For every Hess, who lived to put inmates on report, there was a guard like Buckland, mild and easy and willing to permit even criminals their dignity. Joey liked Buckland far better than McCrory, who spoke only to Gabriel and barely met Joey's eyes at all. Even when they passed in the hall, McCrory physically shrank away, increasing the distance between himself and Joey whenever possible.

"Is that a fresh deck?" Gabriel asked, pointing at the cards in Buckland's hand. Joey knew Gabriel well enough to know when the other man was feigning interest. After work detail, supper and their library rendezvous, Gabriel wanted only to read for a time, then sleep. But when the guards asked for a game, he never said no.

Joey watched for a while, but this game of five-card draw soon went just like the others. Buckland started strong, grew overconfident, and declined to fold once too often, losing an enormous pot to Gabriel. McCrory plodded along with exquisite care, sometimes gaining an excellent hand, only to be disappointed by how quickly Gabriel and Buckland folded. At other times, McCrory would sit up proudly, nodding and smiling, only to have Gabriel instantly call, revealing that McCrory held a pair of deuces or worse.

"Right. I'm off to G-block," Buckland sighed, rising. "Wish they'd let us play you cons for real coin. I'd play better for real coin." He left, but McCrory made no move to follow.

"I don't understand." McCrory sounded so peeved, Joey looked up from his letter, which had progressed no farther than, *Dear Julia, I can't possibly think how to begin ...*

"I've read three books on poker. I understand the game top to bottom. It's not possible I should lose so often." McCrory frowned at Gabriel. "I know Bucky wouldn't cheat. You're not cheating, are you, Gabe?"

Gabriel snorted. "Don't have to. Go read another book. Try me again in the morning."

"Oh." McCrory stared at Gabriel, then sighed. "I'm hopeless, aren't I? Right. Tell me why."

Gathering his winnings – a pile of loose cigarettes – into a battered old tin, Gabriel made a dismissive noise.

"Come on, Gabe. Please. I want to know what you think," McCrory insisted. "I respect you."

Gabriel's hands stopped gathering Pall Malls. He straightened so suddenly, Joey put his letter aside. Something about Gabriel, about his abrupt readiness, reminded Joey of that frozen moment before Gabriel plunged the nail in Paulie's eye. But when Gabriel spoke, his tone was mild.

"You don't respect me." Sweeping the last cigarette into the tin, Gabriel resealed it.

"Of course I do."

"No, you don't. Nor do you want to hear what I have to say on the matter." Gabriel's face went cold.

McCrory appeared so stunned, so helpless, Joey almost felt sorry for him. The guard, no more than thirty, had watery blue eyes and a weak chin. Despite his broad shoulders and considerable heft, there was something childlike about the man, now that Joey took the time to see him.

Gabriel's stern look softened. "Bill. You'll never play poker worth a damn 'til you learn to take risks. It's always the same – you never raise unless you're sure and you're always too timid to call. As for a poker face – Jesus, pigtailed girls playing Old Maid are tougher to read. The entire story of Bill McCrory is written across his mug." Gabriel pointed at the guard with his dog-end. "Including whether he has a bad hand and why he sticks his nose in my cell every night."

Joey caught his breath. He didn't know how to intervene, or if he should try. He wasn't even sure Gabriel was truly angry, or if he spoke harshly only to make himself understood.

"I – it's nothing personal," McCrory said, drawing in his breath. "But it's a rule. Prisoners are not permitted to—"

"Prisoners are not permitted to wager more than one pound sterling's worth of goods in any single game of chance," Gabriel snapped, quoting the Wentworth Prisoners' Handbook. "What do you think we just did? Shall I run to Governor Sanderson and bleat about how you and Buckland tempt me into wickedness?"

"I never mean to tempt—"

"And I never meant to tempt you," Gabriel cut across him. "If you want what I have so badly, go and get it! But I'm sick to death of you spying on me, hoping to get a peek at what you haven't the guts to try!"

McCrory sucked in his breath. For a moment he stared at Gabriel. Then he squared his shoulders and left without another word.

When they heard his heavy footsteps pounding down the stairs, Gabriel turned to Joey. "And now I just bet the whole goddamn pot. Why did you not stop me?"

"Not sure I could have." Joey forced a smile to hide how shaken he was. Plenty of inmates shouted at guards, insulted them, took a swing at them. And those inmates always paid the price, either overtly or by more subtle means. "How did you know? About McCrory, I mean."

"Ah, well, you play cards with a man long enough, you learn who he is. At first I didn't understand.

Not 'til I realized he couldn't look you in the eye. Thirty years old, no wife, no girl I ever heard of. I should have guessed sooner." Gabriel sighed, passing a hand over his face. "And spoke gentler."

The overhead lights snapped off. "We still have ten minutes!" someone bawled. By Joey's watch it was fewer than five, but he'd been at Wentworth long enough to understand the sentiment. It was hard to feel like a man when bedtimes were enforced and sometimes changed on a whim.

"Joey. If McCrory comes back with the lieutenant governor, say I forced you. Beg for a transfer to a different cell block," Gabriel said. "'Twill save you from the lash. We can mend things later."

Joey couldn't see Gabriel's expression in the sudden darkness, but he could imagine it. Hard, stubborn and used to being obeyed. "No."

"We'll still be able to meet. I can still keep you safe. Tell them—"

"I said no." Joey slid his arms around Gabriel, pressing his face against his chest and holding him tight. "If you get the lash, so do I. Let's go to bed."

"At least sleep up in your own bunk. If the lieutenant governor—"

"Gabe. The die is cast. And if I'm due for the lash, I damn sure mean to earn it."

Joey woke twice in the night, dreaming of torches and unlocked doors, but McCrory never reappeared. Later the next day, word went round the cafeteria that McCrory's mum had taken ill and he'd gone home to Clerkenwell to keep vigil at her bedside. Gabriel frowned.

"What is it?" Joey asked.

"His mum's been dead for ages," Gabriel whispered. "Hope the damn fool isn't planning something drastic."

"You could write him a letter. Say things were said in anger. Maybe he's just afraid to face you."

"Inmates cannot post letters or packages to Wentworth staff, or vice versa," Gabriel said. "To prevent the exchange of contraband. For a man who reads as much as you, I don't know why you won't learn the handbook. And how's your own letter coming along?"

"I'm finishing it tonight," Joey said firmly, still uncertain of what he would actually say. "Hell or high water."

But an hour after supper, he still had nothing, just a fountain pen and a fresh sheet of paper. Exasperated with himself, Joey thought, *I'm literate. University educated. And an Englishman, for heaven's sake. I can speak to anyone, under any circumstances, without rudeness or undue emotion. It's in my blood!*

Taking up his pen, he drew in a deep breath and wrote,

Dear Julia,
I hope this letter finds you well. It has been

unseasonably warm here this autumn but with so little rain, that is perhaps to be expected.

I am well settled in my new routine. I work in the gardens most days and have ample quiet time at night. I am ...

Joey paused, putting his pen to his mouth and nibbling thoughtfully on the end. After a moment's consideration he couldn't resist continuing.

... fortunate to have a cellmate whose company I enjoy. He shares many of my interests, including my love of reading. I expect when I leave here, my mind will be improved beyond recognition.

I hope you are quite comfortable in your cousin's house. Life in London should suit you well and permit you to move in new circles. Never doubt that I think well of you and wish you the very best.

Your friend,

Joey

Before he could second-guess himself, Joey folded the letter and placed it in an envelope. There was no point sealing it; it would be read by the prison censors for approval before posting.

As autumn passed into winter, Joey grew more and more accustomed to life at Wentworth. McCrory returned after ten days' absence, thinner, quieter, and no longer inclined to prowl F-block after lights out. Buckland's wife gave birth to a son; he passed out cigars to several inmates, including Joey and Gabriel. Mr. Cranston wanted to renovate his old hothouse, long disused because of broken windows, but was denied permission due to the high cost of plate glass.

Joey suggested the gardener look into old daguerreotype plates, as Lionel Coates had done back home. Sure enough, they could be obtained cheaply, as long as no one objected to ghostly images of unsmiling men and women in the mismatched panes. So Joey spent November helping another inmate repave the hothouse floor as Gabriel shored up the rafters and installed the new windows. It was the first time they'd shared a work detail. Several times each day, often for no particular reason, Joey caught himself looking at Gabriel, usually up a ladder with a hammer in his hand. It was nice to be together in the fresh air, especially with the promise of an undisturbed night to come.

On 12 December, F-block inmates were allowed visitors from noon until two o'clock. Gabriel, expecting his usual visit from Rebecca Eisenberg, queued up with the other men, most of whom awaited wives or mothers. Joey, reading in the unlocked cell, looked up in surprise when Buckland called, "Cooper! You have a visitor! Miss Pearce."

Cooing and whistling broke out amongst the men as Joey hurried to join them. It cut off as Gabriel looked around, startled.

"It's Julia," Joey called.

"Grand." Gabriel's smile showed too many teeth. Turning, he trained his gaze straight ahead, following the man ahead of him.

The visitors' room overlooked the gardens, currently nothing but barren earth and clumps of old snow. Joey found Julia right away, sitting at the very last table. Her blond hair was thicker than he remembered, the natural wave threatening to escape those neat pin curls. The visitors' room was very warm, stuffy even, but Julia wore her coat. Not the slim, stylish wrap he remembered but something large and shapeless, unrefined as a horse blanket. Joey dimly recalled Cousin Dora as big-boned and dowdy. Was Julia dressing to please her hostess?

"Hallo." Joey sat down across from her. The greeting sounded absurd, but it was all he could manage as he looked into Julia's face. She was made up, of course, with sooty eyelashes and a swipe of rouge on her cheeks. But her painted red lips pulled down at the corners no matter how valiantly she tried to smile.

"Joey. Are you quite well?"

His smile, at least, was genuine. It had been so long since anyone addressed him in that once-familiar manner – the unmistakable cadence of an educated person – he was overcome with gratitude.

"Perfectly well, thank you. Did you get my letter?"

Julia nodded. She was as lovely as ever. Those brown eyes stared at Joey as if he'd returned from the dead.

"I must apologize for mine," she said stiffly, as if repeating words long rehearsed. "It was never meant to be sent. I was just pouring out my feelings. My confusion. But Dora took it and posted it and said done was done. And—" Julia looked away, swallowing.

"And the truth is, I was relieved. I thought the cord was cut. That I'd never see or speak to you again."

"Julia, I told you before I was sentenced. Our engagement ceased the moment I was convicted. I understand how important loyalty is to you." Joey wished Julia would look at him, but didn't dare reach across the table for her hand. If she cried out or made any sign of distress, the guards would advance and their visit would conclude, no questions asked. "But I've released you from your promise. I'm happy you've started a new life."

Julia blinked twice, eyes filling with tears. "Oh, God. You mean that, don't you? I came here to beg your forgiveness but now I don't think I can – can—"

"Julia." Casting a quick look at the guards, Joey passed a clean cotton handkerchief across the table. "If you go to pieces, they'll assume I'm to blame and escort you out. So please, be strong. Don't cry."

Seizing the handkerchief, Julia gave a quick, violent nod. As she stared at an imaginary point in space, fighting back tears, Joey glanced across the room. At the front sat Gabriel with a heavyset, plain woman who could only be Rebecca Eisenberg. Her magenta dress clung to her in all the wrong spots; the peacock feather on her hat drooped sadly. But the animated way she moved her hands while talking to Gabriel, eyes alight, confirmed Joey's suspicions.

Joey was surprised by the tightness in his chest. Of course Rebecca Eisenberg was charmed by her former client. Gabriel was younger, fit and handsome. That Irish lilt could make even a dirty word sound poetic, turn even a snarl half-romantic.

"Joey. I'm better now. Thank you." Julia dabbed at the corners of her eyes.

"I'm glad," Joey said, attention shifting back to his former fiancée. After watching Gabriel with Rebecca, he suddenly saw Julia not through the filter of memory but with acute new eyes. She was overheated in her shapeless coat, yet kept it on. Two new lines had formed across her once-smooth brow. She looked tired and frightened, complexion shining with feverish vitality.

"Oh, God," Joey whispered. After adapting to Wentworth he'd believed nothing could startle him, but for a split second, Joey was shaken all the same. Then he cast about within, locating his physician self and pulling it out of mothballs.

"Julia. We've known one another for a long time. But I'm also a doctor. If there's anything you want to confide in me ...," Joey paused, holding her gaze. "There's nothing I haven't heard before. Nothing you can say will shock me."

Ironically, it had been Dr. Pfiser himself who taught Joey that phrase, explaining that even the most frightened woman would relent if such words were spoken kindly enough. And true to Dr. Pfiser's wisdom, Julia's shoulders sagged with relief.

"I – I'm five months gone. Perhaps six," she said, opening her coat enough for Joey to see the curve of her belly within. "And he won't marry me. He's married already. He won't leave his wife for me."

Joey nodded, waiting to feel betrayed, to feel angry. During their long courtship, Julia had permitted him certain liberties, but intercourse had been out of the question. She'd been saving herself for their wedding night, and he'd accepted her decision. Yet as Joey gazed on Julia, all he could think of was Gabriel – nights of mutual need when falling asleep in Gabriel's arms had been the greatest comfort in the world. Surely Julia had craved the same. She'd once loved Joey, he had no doubt of it, yet lost him through no sin of her own. Practically alone in London, existing under a cloud of disgrace, was it any surprise she'd sought comfort in a new man?

"I didn't know Frank was married," Julia whispered, eyes wide, desperate to make Joey understand. "He was separated from his wife and l—li-lied ..." She broke off, controlling herself. "I thought we'd be married. That he was a good man. But once he knew I was ... was—" Julia stopped again, shaking her head and clutching the borrowed handkerchief tight.

Joey glanced at the guards. Neither was paying them the slightest attention. His eyes flicked to Gabriel. The other man stared back at him with hooded eyes and compressed lips. But the moment their gazes locked, Gabriel turned back to Rebecca, beaming his most charming smile.

"What about Dora?" Joey asked. "Does she know?"

Julia's laugh was alarmingly high-pitched. "Of course. Two women can't live together without one knowing if the other's monthly visitor doesn't call. Dora gave me six weeks to change Frank's mind. But the day I started to show, she put me out."

"What?"

"I'm staying at the Nautilus Hotel. It's not terrible. Very modern. The manager never asks questions. I couldn't be luckier. Joey," Julia said suddenly, reaching across the table to take his hand. "When you're released, you can start over. Men can do that; they can marry and start a family at any age. When I read your letter, when I felt how good and honest you were, I knew I had to come. To prove how lucky you are to be shut of me."

Joey blinked. "Bollocks."

"What?" Julia sniffed, startled.

"I never heard anything so - so medieval," Joey said. "Nor so perfectly foolish. You fell in love with a man. He lied to you. Now you're ...," Joey forced his voice lower, "you're going to have a baby. This isn't a penny dreadful, Julia. It's the history of half the human race." Squeezing her hands, Joey stared into her frightened eyes. "If you weren't six months gone, you might have another option. It's very clandestine, mind you, very secret—"

"No." Julia shook her head. "I wouldn't have that on my conscience, even if it were possible. I think perhaps God has something different in mind. That perhaps He's ...," her gaze slid away, "calling me to Him. Me and the baby."

"Julia."

Her head jerked up, shocked by the authority in Joey's voice.

"If there is a God, which I doubt, He didn't do this to you. And the last thing He wants is for a healthy young woman to give up her life before it's begun. If we concentrate," Joey said more gently, still holding her hand, "we can devise a plan. A way for you to go forward."

"I won't go home to my mother," Julia said defiantly. "Dora wrote her a letter. I'll throw myself off a roof before I face Mum now. Besides, the village turned on you, Joey. I despise them for it, I always will."

"Julia. Did you tell everyone we were finished?"

She shook her head.

"Do they understand Wentworth's rules? That you couldn't even visit before now?"

"No."

Joey leaned back in his chair, thinking hard. "Right. First. Go to the guard. Ask for a pen and paper. Write down your address and telephone exchange for me. And I may not be able to contact you directly, so be sure to accept any message from Wentworth."

Joey and Gabriel ate supper in uncharacteristic silence. The meal was enlivened only by Lonnie, who seemed uncomfortable when more than a minute ticked by without someone speaking. The meal was boiled fish, prompting Lonnie to compose a poem that rhymed "Joey Cooper" with "tasty grouper." When Gabriel ignored that, Lonnie challenged him to arm wrestling, struggling comically against Gabriel's most gentle pressure. By the time Joey and Gabriel returned to their unlocked cell, the unspoken tension had mostly dissipated. Then Joey opened their small cupboard and drew out his copy of the Wentworth

Prisoners' Handbook. Until now he'd refused to read it, believing that the moment he did, he accepted his lot. But suppose it contained the answers he needed?

Joey read until lights out, plowing through page after page without any luck. The handbook was haphazardly organized, Wentworth's rules and regulations enumerated in the order the authors remembered them. Once they were plunged into darkness, Joey considered asking Gabriel for the electric torch, then thought better of it. Gabriel hadn't enjoyed seeing Joey with Julia. And Joey hadn't liked watching Gabriel flirt with Rebecca Eisenberg. Demanding use of the torch would be asking for a fight.

"Well?" Gabriel demanded, already stripped and stretched out on the bottom bunk.

"Well, what?" Joey shrugged out of his shirt. His pajamas remained folded in the cupboard; he never bothered with them anymore.

"What act of God or man prompted you to crack the handbook?"

"I was wondering." Joey stepped out of his trousers. Peeling off his shorts, he slid into Gabriel's warm, hard embrace, closing his eyes as the other man kissed him.

"Wondering what?"

Joey pulled back, squinting as he tried to see Gabriel's face in the gloom. "If the governor would allow me to get married."

It took considerable effort to secure permission, but Joey was determined. First he petitioned the lieutenant governor, then Wentworth's chaplain, then Governor Sanderson himself, who initially declined to see Joey. It was Gabriel's suggestion – dropping the name Rebecca Eisenberg – that turned the tide. Her organization British Women for Prison Reform was always looking into prisoner complaints, bombarding the Home Office with letters, phone calls, and threats of legal action. Governor Sanderson was already fighting Rebecca on two fronts: "slopping out" and corporal punishment. He was in no hurry to add a third.

"You understand this is most irregular," Governor Sanderson began. A big, bullish man with salt-and-pepper hair, he was the sort whose coat and tie always looked rumpled, even at ten in the morning.

"I do." Since coming to Wentworth, Joey had fallen back on his boyhood speech patterns in an effort to fit in. Now he deliberately took up his Oxford manner, the crisper dialect that allowed him to mix with children of privilege. "But you understand time is of the essence. While awaiting trial I behaved badly. Now my fiancée has presented me with the consequences. Perhaps she, like I, deserves the social punishment that must come. But not the child." Pausing, Joey held Governor Sanderson's gaze. "The child has done nothing wrong. Yet he'll grow up a bastard, as I did.

And perhaps find himself here, as I have, after formative years without a good name to call his own."

The argument was more nonsense than truth. Joey wasn't bitter over his boyhood. He'd had his looks and his wits; so many other children had neither, and the stain of illegitimacy to boot. But Gabriel had explained the men in charge of Wentworth wouldn't be moved by the pleas of a fornicating couple – one of them a convict – suddenly desperate for the sacrament of marriage. Only by invoking the innocent unborn child could Joey hope to secure permission. And true to Gabriel's prediction, Governor Sanderson relented.

After another meeting to determine the logistics, Joey and Julia were permitted to wed in Wentworth's small chapel. The ceremony took place on a Sunday evening at eight thirty. To Joey's relief, none of the inmates were permitted to attend. It was odd enough, marrying a former lover in Wentworth's poky little chapel while the lieutenant governor and Governor Sanderson looked on, both dressed in the dark suits they wore to executions. Adding Gabriel's cold eyes and false smile to the occasion would have rendered it unbearable.

After signing the necessary documents, Joey and Julia were led to Wentworth's visitors' hall, where family members of dying or condemned inmates were permitted to temporarily reside. They were given a room with a double bed, a bathtub and a flushing toilet. The guard stationed outside the unlocked door would allow them to remain until six o'clock. Then Joey would be escorted back to F-block and Julia would exit Wentworth as Mrs. Joseph Cooper.

"I'm sorry I wore such a tent," Julia said, meaning her enormous A-line shift, as soon as they were alone. "But since I'm meant to be eight months pregnant, I wanted to look the part."

"You're lovely." Joey sat down on the foot of the bed, clasping his hands on his lap.

"So it's real. We're married." Julia sat down on the other side. For a little while she was silent. Then, seeming to realize the distance between them, she scooted an inch closer to Joey. "Thank you."

Julia was still blushing from their brief, ceremonial kiss. So was he. Joey tried to think of something to say, but nothing came to him as they studied one another across their marriage bed.

Next morning, Joey returned to the cell by a quarter after six, but Gabriel was already gone. Expecting to find the other man in the cafeteria, Joey went through the line, choosing rubbery eggs and fried bread, only to realize Gabriel wasn't at any of the tables. After breakfast, Joey reported to Mr. Cranston, who congratulated him on his nuptials before setting Joey to repotting seedlings. By midwinter Wentworth's cafeteria would gain a glorious infusion of herbs and spices.

Joey didn't see Gabriel at dinner or supper. Nor was he embroiled in the card games during common time.

Frustrated, Joey finally went to their cell and found the other man at the table, Bible open to the Book of Revelations.

"I've been looking for you." Joey smiled. Gabriel didn't look up.

"Sure and you've found me."

Joey sat down across from Gabriel. A minute passed, silent, excruciating.

"Gabe. Don't tell me you're planning to read the goddamn Bible all night long."

The other man's eyes flicked up. "Surely you didn't just mock the word of God and take the Lord's name in vain all in one breath."

"I mocked you, not the word of God," Joey said firmly. "As for taking the Lord's name in vain – I've news for you, you're just as guilty, even if you always pronounce it 'Jay-sus.'"

Gabriel closed his Bible. Lifting his chin, he gave Joey a tight smile. "You're right. I should say sorry. I've no call to be rude, I'm just jealous. I'll never bed another woman. How was it? Spare me no details."

Joey stood up. Going to the bucket, he had a piss. After, Joey washed his hands in the basin and splashed water on his face. He knew what he would do. He'd change into his pajamas, climb into the top bunk and resume reading *Lost Horizon*. He was sharing it with Gabriel, as Wentworth's library had only one copy. And just let Gabriel object. Let him say one word, make one sound, and then they'd have it out. Then Joey would—

Joey glanced at Gabriel. The Bible was open to the same page; he was only pretending to read. And the first two fingers of his right hand were more yellowed than ever. He'd been smoking up a storm.

Joey stepped behind Gabriel. He meant to put his hands on Gabriel's shoulders and whisper "You Irish ass" in his ear. The last time they'd quarreled, over some miniscule issue only two men sharing a locked cell could find worthy of dispute, that phrase had made Gabriel relent.

Joey expected resistance, even a halfhearted blow. But the moment his hands touched Gabriel's shoulders, the other man relaxed. This was a new power of Joey's, one that seemed to deepen each day – to soften Gabriel, to disarm him with a touch.

"I love you," Joey heard himself say. It surprised him, frightened him and made him desperately happy, all at once.

Gabriel drew in his breath. Then he stood up, turning in a blink and pulling Joey close. "Say it again."

Joey's heart was pounding fast. Being held by Gabriel still thrilled him to the marrow. "I love you, you great Irish ass."

Gabriel kissed him. Joey was pushing his tongue into the other man's mouth when he heard Buckland call, "Oh, for Chrissake! MacKenna, Cooper, none of that! Let the lieutenant governor see and you'll both get the lash!"

Buckland strolled up to the open cell as Gabriel pulled his face away, still holding Joey in his arms. "And you a newlywed, Cooper. For shame," Buckland added without real censure.

"Shame? Here's what I say to that." Gabriel dipped

Joey all way back, supporting him as if they were on a dance floor instead of a prison. Then he kissed Joey, open-mouthed, as the nearest inmates burst into applause.

Buckland walked off shaking his head. "I'd write my memoir, but nobody would believe it."

After lights out and the nightly bed check, Gabriel climbed into Joey's bunk. Already engorged and unable to wait, he threw a leg over Joey and had him, thrusts deep, swift and desperate. Coming hard, Gabriel fell into Joey's arms, kissing the other man's throat and whispering to him in Gaelic.

"You've said those words before," Joey murmured. Gabriel had gone too fast for Joey to climax, but his turn would come. And to be needed so urgently meant more than his personal satisfaction, anyway. "What do they mean?"

"My own love." Gabriel traced a finger along Joey's hairline, pushing an errant strand back in place. "My only love."

Joey shifted, turning in Gabriel's arms so they fit like spoons. Gabriel dug his fingers into Joey's hair, running his nails along the scalp with delicate, tantalizing scrapes until Joey gave a little moan. Then Gabriel was kneading Joey's shoulders, working the knotted muscles. Those callused, long-fingered hands felt so good, Joey's cock stiffened. His asshole, slick with cum and still throbbing from hard use, clenched with a sublime mixture of pain and pleasure. Then Gabriel's hands slid over his nipples, twisting each nub between thumb and forefinger until Joey stifled a groan.

"My cock," he whispered, trying to pull Gabriel's hand down.

"No. I took you too fast. Now I'll build you up slow." Gabriel caressed Joey's belly, pressing and stroking until Joey's back arched with frustrated need. He could have used his own hand – he was dying to use his own hand – but it felt maddeningly good, writhing in Gabriel's embrace. Rubbing his ass against the other man's thigh, Joey brought on more waves of pain/pleasure as he waited ... waited ...

"Oh," Joey gasped as Gabriel's hand finally closed around his cock. Bucking along with the motion, Joey pushed his ass against Gabriel's thigh. He arched once, twice, three times before he splattered the wall with hot, salt-smelling cum.

For a long time afterward they lay quietly, Joey luxuriating in the heat of Gabriel's arms. Gabriel was stroking him again, just a gentle trace of fingertips along his forearm.

"Gabe, I love you," Joey whispered, turning to face the other man. "Last night. After the ceremony. Julia and I, we—"

Gabriel interrupted with a grunt. "No. 'Tis none of my business. I had no right to ask such a thing. If you'd taken a swing, I wouldn't have come back at you."

"—we talked, Gabe. She's still in love with Frank. That's why she went so far, got herself into trouble – she loved him. Probably more than she ever loved me. We were childhood sweethearts, you know. What we had was more innocence than real passion. And even though Frank left, she – she won't heal easily. Not 'til the baby comes."

"You mean ...?"

"We did nothing but talk." Joey rose on one elbow to meet Gabriel's stare. "She told me about Frank and I told her about you."

Gabriel's eyes widened. "Jesus."

"Didn't I warn you about taking the Lord's name in vain?" Kissing Gabriel's lips, Joey lay down again. "Julia's a terribly honest person. It would have destroyed her to pretend she still loved me. Bad enough she has to go home to my mum and lie to her. But it's all for the best. My mum's a soft touch. She'll imagine she sees my face in the baby's no matter what. And she'll be overjoyed, and glad to have the little tyke around, which is all that matters."

After that they kissed, talked and dozed without really sleeping. Having now said "I love you" three times, Joey found he couldn't stop saying it. And every time he did, Gabriel was more inflamed, kissing and stroking him as if they hadn't fucked only a few hours before. Joey was increasingly aroused by the smell of sweat and cum, the taste of tobacco, the whisper of filthy Gaelic in his ear. Gabriel was half-up despite the fact he usually needed a day's recovery, but Joey was hard as a crowbar all over again.

"Gabe. Let me fuck you," he whispered.

"Swore I'd never allow that."

"You want it."

"Oh, aye," Gabriel said, feeling in the bedclothes for the lubricant.

Coating two fingers with clear jelly, Joey pressed them between Gabriel's legs. As he expected, the other man evinced no pain, no matter how insistently Joey fought to loosen him. But as he worked a third finger into the tight, hot space, Gabriel began to tremble, catching his breath. Each time Joey pushed the spongy tissue, Gabriel choked back a moan. And when Joey pulled his fingers away, the moan burst free. Gabriel was panting, eyes wide.

"Gabe. On your belly."

Gabriel obeyed. Taking the other man by the hips, Joey drove his cock down that slick channel, sheathing himself in one thrust. Gabriel shuddered with obvious pleasure; Joey, half out of his body with the sensation, pumped in and out with terrible urgency. Forever wouldn't have been long enough. When Gabriel seized, Joey left himself entirely, flesh overloaded with pleasure, spirit suspended between life and death.

"Joey? Are you all right?"

Drawing a deep breath, Joey opened his eyes. "Never better. You?"

"'Twas sweet." Gabriel smiled. "And I was thinking. Now that we've both had each other – that's as good as taking vows, isn't it?"

Julia delivered a girl on March 11, 1937. Joey wasn't permitted to visit them in the hospital, but she brought the baby – Lily – on the next visitors' day in June. There was no way for Gabriel to have a look at the child himself – in the visitors' room, moving from table to table was strictly forbidden. If Gabriel so much as stood up without permission, his visit with Rebecca Eisenberg would be terminated.

"The key to a new world for women," Rebecca was saying as Gabriel made one last attempt to get a look at the bundle in Julia's arms.

"Hmnh?" Gabriel blinked, realizing he'd lost the thread.

"Abortion," Rebecca said in the same firm, unflinching tone she would have said "sunbeam." "Stella Browne says the legalization of abortion is the key to women having the same freedoms as men."

Gabriel frowned. "How did we come to that topic?"

"You asked what my focus for the summer would be. Since I've yet to make any real progress in your world with regards to the birch, the cat-o'-nine tails or even the slop bucket." Rebecca's large brown eyes shone with affection. "I don't have to ask what your focus is."

Gabriel passed Rebecca a cigarette. As usual, she reached for the matches; as usual, he stayed her hand, lighting it for her with a smile. "I don't suppose you found anything?"

"No. The case was properly tried and defended. None of the evidence is suspect. No hint the witnesses were tampered with. And your friend admitted to writing the confession, albeit dictated. That written confession will be impossible to overcome unless Dr. Pfiser is publicly disgraced."

"Is that likely?"

Rebecca shook her head. "Dr. Pfiser had a stroke

just after the new year. Retired from active practice. So there's no hope he'll botch another case and throw Dr. Cooper's conviction into question."

Gabriel clenched a fist. "It eats at me, Rebecca. Joey's a good man. Finest man I know. For him to rot here, mucking about with wheelbarrows and shrubbery when he has a wife ...... a child ..."

"I thought you said the marriage was a sham," Rebecca said, still in the firm, carrying tone.

Gabriel cleared his throat, glancing around to make sure no one had heard. "'Tis true. But he was meant to wed her before he was stitched up. Before his life was stolen. Seeing Joey with her and the babe ..." Gabriel exhaled a plume of smoke. "There must be something that can be done."

Rebecca studied him. "You know, in our correspondence, Dr. Cooper seems quite diffident about last-ditch legal ploys. He seems to have accepted his sentence. In fact, he strikes me as more keen to know what might be done for you."

Gabriel closed his eyes, shaking his head and holding back a curse because he was in the presence of a lady. "I've told him before. I was meant for the gallows. Sparing my life is the most anyone can expect of the Crown. I'll be here 'til I'm a doddering old man, eating nothing but mush and sh—soiling my uniform like poor old Hansen," he said, referring to a man convicted in 1888. Too old for work detail and utterly harmless, Hansen now spent his days propped beside a window, dreaming of an outside world long vanished.

Rebecca looked sad. Realizing he might have

sounded ungrateful, Gabriel added, "Then again, who says I'll live so long? Both my uncles died of the cancer. A nephew, too."

"Cancer? Which sort?"

"Lung. Hard luck. Then again, all three spent the better part of their lives in London. Terrible air off the Thames." Gabriel took another deep drag from his cigarette. "Rebecca. I don't mean to badger you on the subject. But, please – if you come across any reform act that might help Joey, let me know. Not him. Me."

As 1937 stretched into 1938, then 1939, Wentworth changed less than it stayed the same. Governor Sanderson announced that A-block, crumbling at its foundations and overrun with rats and rising damp, would be completely renovated by 1941. As usual, Gabriel would oversee a good part of the labor, though with fewer materials than ever before. Rumors of a second world war, inconceivable as it might be after the horrors of the first, had Governor Sanderson scrambling to requisition building materials before the Home Office froze all requests.

In 1938 Benjamin Stiles went to the infirmary for an infected cut on his great toe and died, prompting several vicious newspaper articles and a lawsuit from British Women for Prison Reform. The official story was, the big man suffered from an enlarged heart that suddenly gave out. True or untrue, the public was moved by the account of Stiles' mild nature and mental deficiency. A scapegoat was demanded, and Dr. Royal was dismissed from his position at long last.

Early in 1939 Hess caught Lonnie fellating his cellmate and reported the incident to the lieutenant governor. The next day, Lonnie, crying and pleading, was tied to a rectangular frame and given fifteen lashes with the cat-o'-nine tails. All the prisoners were assembled to watch. Joey pushed toward the front to provide moral support. Gabriel remained in the very back, arms tight across his chest, eyes on floor.

After his recovery, Lonnie was transferred to F-block. Arriving whey-faced and scrawny as a stray dog, he perked up only when one of the inmates whispered something in his ear.

"Is it true? Hess is dead?" Lonnie asked Joey, incredulous.

Joey nodded. Buckland and McCrory were out of earshot, embroiled as usual in a card game with Gabriel. Still, Joey drew Lonnie all the way into his unlocked cell before explaining, "Hess slipped in the showers."

"And *died*?"

"Well, the rumor is, he fell on his face. There's a bone here," Joey said, touching the bridge of Lonnie's nose, right at the top. "A sharp, shift blow will send it into the brain. Hess was unlucky, that's all."

It took Lonnie some time to digest that. Then he started to shake all over, half-crying and half-laughing. "Dirty bastard had it coming. Joey – you and Gabe are the best friends a man could have."

"Lonnie, I never said – we didn't—" Joey began, alarmed.

"I know," Lonnie said, wiping his nose on his sleeve like a schoolboy. "I'm slow, but I'm no dunce. Hess fell down. Good riddance. And if I can ever pay either of you back, I will."

It was a snowy morning in November 1939 when Buckland showed Gabriel an op-ed piece called "Must Only The Innocent Be Sacrificed?" Written by a minor politician, the article suggested that since Prime Minister Chamberlain had committed Great Britain's young men to fight and die on foreign soil, those less valuable to society should be expected to do the same.

For years we law-abiding citizens have paid to feed, clothe, even entertain the criminal population. Perhaps it's time the malcontents and misfits currently lounging about at His Majesty's pleasure in the warmth and safety of institutions like Wentworth be compelled to take up arms? To redeem themselves in the eyes of their fellow man?

"See? Don't let me hear you complain," Buckland laughed. "You're warm and safe when you could be out fighting the Nazis."

Gabriel thought about the article all day. Even while playing poker, his mind drifted back to it. Before he knew it, McCrory had bluffed him out of everything but the cigarettes in his left breast pocket.

"I should never have given you that lesson at cards," Gabriel said as they exited the common room. "When you see me smoking Bolsheviks from now on, I hope it gives your conscience a nasty turn."

McCrory chuckled. It had taken months for him and Gabriel to rekindle their old friendliness. Lately, McCrory had been smiling a lot, telling lame jokes and overlooking minor infractions. Now he hummed tunelessly to himself as the three men walked down the hall, prompting Buckland to elbow Gabriel.

"Imagining a Christmas cuppa with the lovely Pat, no doubt. That's why Bill's all sweetness and light these days."

McCrory chuckled, shaking his head. He looked so pleased at the ribbing, Gabriel felt compelled to keep it up after Buckland veered away.

"Is that why you took all a poor man's Pall Malls? Your girl smokes 'em out of a long black holder?"

"I never said that." McCrory's gaze flicked up to meet Gabriel's.

"Too much of a lady for the filthy habit?"

"No. I never said Pat was a girl. Everyone's assumed it." McCrory began to redden. "It's been easy to get away with, easier than I ever dreamed. We bought an old duplex and cut a door in the center wall. Our neighbors think nothing of us."

The pleasure in McCrory's eyes left Gabriel uncharacteristically at a loss for words. About to clap the other man on the back and send him on his way, Gabriel suddenly realized why McCrory had confided him. Out of all the men in Wentworth, Gabriel was the only one McCrory could talk to about Pat. And he was bursting at the seams to tell someone.

Over the next two weeks Gabriel learned everything there was to know about Patrick Horton, including his favorite foods, his tendency to snore and his rising prominence in the War Office. This last bit interested Gabriel most of all, though he forced himself to wait a day before showing McCrory the op-ed article about convicts joining the war effort.

Tucking the newspaper under his arm, McCrory promised to ask Pat about it that very evening. Next day, he greeted Gabriel with a shake of the head.

"Pat says it's all politics. Never happen. And to be honest, I think it's a terrible idea." McCrory looked apologetic. "Most of these blighters aren't like you, Gabe. They'd be shot for desertion or banged up all over again for insubordination. Sorry. Do you want out so bad that you'd let the PM ship you away as cannon fodder?"

"Not me. Joey. He's a fully qualified doctor. Surely the Army could use one?"

McCrory sighed. "No offense, but Cooper was convicted for killing two of his patients. Not sure even the Army wants a doctor like that. Hell, I think they'd rather have a master carpenter."

Much later that night, as Joey lay in his arms, Gabriel floated the notion for the first time. The other man's swift, contemptuous dismissal astonished him.

"Bill's right. Getting shipped off to die is worse than serving my time here. Wentworth is lovely – no bullets, no bombs and no country that wadded me up and tossed me in the rubbish bin expecting me to die for her. Besides," Joey lifted himself to stare into

Gabriel's face. "We'd be separated forever. Why would I choose that?"

"I know it's a gamble. But keep your head down, finish your tour and you can start over. Go home to Julia, give her another baby, live your goddamn life."

"And forget you even exist?" Joey's gray eyes were sharp in the torch's muted glow. "You have a martyr complex, you know that?"

"'Course I do. I'm Catholic," Gabriel laughed. He kissed Joey until the other man smiled. "I know you don't like to think on the future. But see reason. If you serve your full sentence, by the time you're out, Julia will be too old to give you more children. You'll be so out of practice as a physician, it might be impossible to take up again. And you and I will still be separated forever. You won't even be able to send me love letters without the censors cutting them to ribbons."

"Gabe. You're a persuasive devil. But you'll never win this one." Joey settled back into Gabriel's arms with a yawn. "The only way I'll leave Wentworth early is if you do, too."

At first Rebecca was energized by the possibility. One of her solicitor friends had it on good authority that if Winston Churchill became prime minister in the next election, MI6 and at least two other government agencies would be combined to fight the Axis on unconventional terms.

"This isn't a scheme to round up cannon fodder for the front lines," Rebecca said. "MI6 is only interested in people with special skills. An Oxford-educated physician certainly fits the bill. But there's no reason they shouldn't consider you, too. This Office of Special Operations, or whatever they finally call it, will need engineers, plumbers and carpenters, too. It isn't just a brain trust."

"Thanks for that," Gabriel said dryly. But inside he was light as a feather. That night he and Joey stayed up most of the night, whispering and laughing softly like boys on a sleepover as they planned what they would do after the war.

"No," Gabriel said firmly. "I'll not have you divorce the poor woman on account of me."

"I never said divorce. Julia and I can live apart. There's a fine old English tradition of remaining married on paper whilst buggering off for greener pastures, old chap," Joey said, putting on the posh tones that always amused Gabriel. "We'll take a flat in the city, tell everyone we're brothers. I'll work on my Irish brogue. I already have Jay-sus down pat."

Over the next three weeks the plans grew more detailed. The flat became a duplex, à la McCrory and Pat. Gabriel would construct a passage between the two living spaces. The bedroom on his side would be for show; the bedroom on Joey's side would be theirs. The idea of making love or even just sleeping whenever he fancied it was particularly tantalizing. As was the notion of using his skills however he wished, not just for construction but for his own pleasure.

"A master carpenter is an artisan, too," he told Joey. "I can carve us a bedstead. A highboy. A sideboard for our kitchen."

"Kitchen?" Joey looked worried. "One of us will have to learn to cook."

They regarded each other, each turning the unfamiliar notion over in his head.

"We'll bring in a woman for that," Gabriel said at last.

"She'll know all our business."

"Aye, and she'll not give a damn if we pay a good wage. Will it be hard for you to find work as a doctor?"

"I don't know. Worst case, I can join a charity. I shan't be idle, that's for certain. And in my spare time," Joey smiled, "I'll work in our garden."

But when Gabriel next met Rebecca Eisenberg, it wasn't in the visitors' room. It was an official meeting in her capacity as his solicitor. She put on a brave smile, rising to take both his hands, but the moment Gabriel looked in her eyes he knew the news wasn't good.

"You can't tell me they don't need physicians," he gasped, too amazed to be angry. "They'll let a man like Joey rot rather than win this war?"

"Actually – Dr. Cooper has already been accepted. If he agrees to work for the War Office until the war ends or until he's deemed unfit for service, his sentence will be commuted. He'll even be eligible for a pension."

Gabriel laughed. "Why – that's wonderful. Perfect!"

"They considered you, too, Gabriel. But after they

read the transcripts from your trial ..." Rebecca broke off, shaking her head.

Gabriel was surprised at his own disappointment. He hadn't really believed it. Surely he'd just played along with Joey, building castles in the air as yet another way to tempt the other man into understanding just what was being offered. Still, for the first time Gabriel suffered a stab of fear. What would his life in Wentworth be like without Joey?

Gabriel swallowed the thought. God knew there'd been times in his life when he'd lost his way. But when he recognized the right path he'd take it, and the cost be damned.

"Of course they won't have me. I'm a double murderer, no matter what you got the Crown to call it."

Rebecca sighed. "No. It was the psychiatrist's testimony. The same testimony that saved your life. That, along with your family medical history."

Gabriel winced, waving Rebecca into silence. Everyone knew madness ran on his mother's side. He'd admitted as much to Joey, though he'd left out the particulars – the cousins who'd heard voices, the aunt who'd strangled her own babe, believing it possessed of the devil. But to hear a learned man state plainly from the witness box that Gabriel had suffered a psychotic break – that when he committed the murders, he'd been unable to distinguish right from wrong, or reality from fantasy – still hurt even ten years later. The psychiatrist, a white-haired man in a pinstriped suit, had explained that several factors, including Gabriel's inability to flee afterward, to explain why he'd erupted or even recognize his brother Joseph, proved he'd been insane at the time. Or, since the Crown did not recognize temporary insanity, "possessed by irresistible impulse."

Rebecca Eisenberg and her cronies had nodded in sympathy. So had the foreman of the jury. But Gabriel, sickened by his diagnosis, had prayed the court would declare him a wicked man and put him to death.

"I'm sorry, Gabriel." Rebecca's tone was as firm and direct as ever, but her large brown eyes were soft.

"No need to be sorry. You've given me wonderful news. And what you've done for Joey – it's a star in your heavenly crown, I promise. Far better than saving my neck."

"I'll be the judge of that," Rebecca sighed. But she tried to look happy all the same.

Joey took the news just as Gabriel feared. He refused to go. He wasn't interested in the particulars, didn't care about the commuted sentence, the pension, the fact he'd be no ordinary soldier but a specialist attached to the War Office.

"I won't leave you," Joey said, eyes gleaming precisely as they had when he'd refused to lie, even under threat of the lash. "Think how much the system has changed since you were convicted. By the time I'm ready for release, the Crown might be willing to parole you. Permit some kind of work release. Allow me to visit you, at least, without all these goddamn foolish rules."

"Fine. And Julia? Lily? No husband or father needed for either, is that so?"

Joey shook his head. "I helped Julia. I'll give Lily whatever I can. But I won't cut my throat because another man needs blood. You matter most to me, Gabe. I couldn't sleep at night knowing I'd left you behind."

Gabriel, realizing Joey was immoveable on the subject, wrote Rebecca and asked her to stall the War Office a little longer. The direct approach had failed. If he wanted Joey to take this opportunity, he'd need a more persuasive argument.

The declaration of war changed daily life throughout London. Even at Wentworth, Governor Sanderson's best-laid plans were threatened. Facing the Home Office's edict – any building materials not utilized by April 1, 1940, must be turned back over to the war effort – Governor Sanderson declared that the renovation of A-block would proceed at triple speed. Joey was removed from his customary garden detail to assist with the work, which now stretched over three daily shifts instead of two. Governor Sanderson, it was noted, hated the Nazis as much as any Englishman. But he hated the rats and rising damp in A-block a good deal more.

Gabriel knew Joey wasn't overjoyed with his changed duties, but given the nationwide concern over food stores, Wentworth's own "victory garden" was due for expansion. Joey had drawn up the plans with Mr. Cranston's enthusiastic approval. Once A-block was finished, Joey would surely find himself back in the sunshine again.

Though accustomed to sustained physical labor, Gabriel wasn't used to working from noon 'til nine. Having Joey within sight was also a sweet distraction. Finally, the addition of E-block, including one-eyed Paulie, made even simple bricklaying tedious. Bitter about being compelled to work through what had always been their common time, the E-block men tested the tempers of the guards, the F-block inmates and one another.

Using his blond gorilla arms to hook crates onto steel S-hooks, Paulie hauled up crates with a rope-and-pulley rigging. The roof was still off, the night sky boundless above them, moonless with a smattering of stars. But the men on the half-completed south wall received exactly three crates of materials before Paulie, pleading exhaustion, started bawling for another break. The guards, Buckland and a new man called York, equally resentful of their unpaid extra hours, called a bonus break for everyone. York went off in search of coffee while Buckland bummed a smoke off Gabriel.

"Wish I could join the Army," Paulie announced. Since losing his eye he'd become as mournful as a street corner drunk, bemoaning all the wrongs he'd suffered. He hated Gabriel, hated him so much he could barely look at him, but oddly bore Joey no ill will. Paulie seemed to feel his near-rape of Joey was completely unrelated to the nail to the eye that followed.

"I heard a rumor smart cons like you might be eligible, Cooper," Paulie continued. "Wouldn't you'd like to fight the Nazis?"

"Of course. The minute they turn up at Wentworth." Joey, who always carried a book with him, was sitting beneath one of the dangling klieg lights and trying to read.

"The Army only takes men," Fitch, one of the newer inmates, announced. Big and strong, nearly as wide as he was tall, Fitch was still finding his place at Wentworth. Already he'd been sentenced to the lash, yet seemed unaffected by the experience. He'd taken no girl, sometimes deriding effeminate males like Lonnie, sometimes openly lusting after them. And he was far too interested in Joey. Fitch's fascination had started with stares, whispers, brushing up against Joey in the showers. Tonight it seemed Fitch was progressing to direct remarks. That meant Gabriel would have to put a stop to it soon, as forcefully as possible.

Joey, turning a page, didn't seem to hear Fitch's opinion. Every muscle tensed, Gabriel watched Fitch's small eyes beneath that Cro-Magnon brow, waiting.

"Cooper! Settle a bet for me," Fitch called. "You a boy or a girl?"

"Never mind what's between my legs. You'll be having none of it," Joey said, eyes still on his book.

Gabriel chuckled, loud enough for Fitch to hear.

The big man turned.

"Laughing at me, mate?"

"That I am."

"Steady on." Buckland raised a hand. "We're all friends here. Let's leave off the taunts and enjoy our break."

Fitch's small eyes flicked from Gabriel to Joey and back again. "I hear you girls are married."

Gabriel sucked hard on his cigarette and pitched it aside. "Come closer and say that."

"Oh, for Chrissake, I can't have this," Buckland complained, rubbing his eyes and stifling a yawn. "I don't want to put anyone on the list for birching, but I will if I must! I can, you know! I certainly can!"

"You're too skinny for me, MacKenna," Fitch said. "Rather have a go at your bit of stuff."

Advancing on Joey, Fitch smacked the book out of his hand with something metallic. Gabriel barely had time to realize it was an S-hook before Fitch had the hook's sharp end pressed against Joey's throat.

"Cock or pussy, pretty girl? Give me a feel." Fitch's hand closed over Joey's crotch. "Cock!"

"Fuck you," Joey cried, shoving away the hook with both hands.

"No!" Buckland wailed, fumbling with the baton at his belt.

Gabriel saw it unfold perfectly, like a maestro separating a symphony's unified sound into smaller component parts. Joey gobsmacked Fitch with his right fist while hammering the big man's gut with his left. But Fitch still had the S-hook. It was coming around, coming around fast—

Gabriel was already there. His instincts told him to stop the S-hook with his right hand, catch Fitch's throat with his left and flatten Fitch's bollocks with his knee for good measure. Fitch wasn't faster than Gabriel and he sure as hell wasn't smarter. This bit of defiance would be his last.

But how long can this go on? Gabriel wondered suddenly. Joey was as beautiful now as he'd been almost four years ago. How many times would Gabriel fight this battle? And for what? To keep Joey comfortable at Wentworth, happy, unwilling to leave, content to—

"Oh, God," Gabriel gasped as crushing pain started in his belly and dragged its way up. Fitch grinned happily in Gabriel's face like a schoolboy winning a ribbon. Then another hand seized the S-hook from Fitch—

—Gabriel cried out, the pain blinding as the implement was dislodged from his body—

—and then the S-hook was driven into Fitch's throat. A geyser of crimson erupted.

"Go to hell! You go to hell!" Lonnie was screaming, spattered in red from head to toe.

"Gabe! No!" Joey cried. But Gabriel sank to his knees, watching the weakening jets of blood pump out of Fitch's jugular with dreamlike detachment.

"Gabe." Joey was beside him, weeping. The realization snapped Gabriel back to reality, a place where every voice was too loud, every light too bright. Even his side hurt, as if his rotten appendix had grown back.

"What is it?" Gabriel swiped at Joey's tears. "Are

you hurt?"

"You need to lie back." Even as Joey spoke, he was easing Gabriel onto the ground. Looking at his torso, Gabriel took in what happened – the extent of Fitch's strength, the damage he'd wrought with one sharpened tool. The wound started in Gabriel's belly, a handful of ropy white guts protruding, then arced crookedly up his chest toward his heart. At the midpoint, blood leaked from the wound in thin, quick spurts, already starting to pool beside him.

"Lonnie pulled out the hook. Killed Fitch with it," Gabriel said.

Still weeping, Joey nodded, eyes wide.

"Good on him. Be sure I get the credit. I don't want him hanging on my account. And if they charge you with murder, you'll lose the right to work for the War Office."

Joey made a shocked noise, closing his eyes and shaking his head as if he couldn't believe Gabriel could possibly mention such a thing. But Gabriel felt quite lucid.

"It doesn't hurt much. How long will it take?"

"I think your aorta is nicked. That's the spot that's bleeding so fast. If I'm right ... it won't take long."

"Two men dead," Buckland was moaning, pacing between Gabriel and Fitch and squeezing his head in his hands like a broken man. "Dear God, I won't just get the sack. I'll be up on charges for criminal negligence."

Gabriel never saw Paulie charge the guard, but he recognized Paulie's voice.

"Hard luck, screw. Let me do you a kindness."

There was a wet smack and a thud as Buckland's body hit the ground.

"We're doing a runner!" Paulie cried. "Cooper! MacKenna's a dead man! Come on!"

"The search teams will drag them back. They'll all get the lash, plus another two years. Best to stay," Gabriel whispered. But he knew from the look on Joey's face that the other man wouldn't leave him, not even if an airplane waited just outside.

"Joey. Push my guts in. I can't look at them." Gabriel closed his eyes and waited. But the action hardly hurt at all. Gabriel felt cold and weak, but the pain was nothing next to his bout of appendicitis. When Gabriel dared look at himself again, the wound was no longer grotesque. Just a deep gash and some blood. Distantly, an alarm clanged. Soon floodlights would snap on and obliterate the night sky.

"Joey, I'm afraid," Gabriel said, not because he wanted to, but because he couldn't help himself. "Of dying. Of going to hell."

"There is no hell." Joey lay down against Gabriel's uninjured side as he had after the appendectomy. "There's only Christ."

"I've not been confessed or absolved. He won't have me."

"He will," Joey said with a perfect assuredness Gabriel couldn't disbelieve.

"I'll confess to you, then." Gabriel named his sins simply, with a minimum of words, but Joey, no Catholic, lacked the ritual language to receive them. So after each declaration he kissed Gabriel's lips, whispering the same response, "I love you. I love you.

I love you."

Gabriel wanted to make Joey promise to enlist, to survive the war and live his life thereafter, but his vision was fading; it was too much effort to speak. He wanted to say the things Joey had said just before he was taken to St. George's, the words that had meant so much: *I've gone with you as far as I can. I'll be waiting for you.* But "I love you" was all Gabriel heard, all he felt, all he was.

Joey studied himself in the lavatory mirror. He had to admit, he looked sharp in uniform. He wished Gabriel could see him.

He hadn't been allowed to attend Gabriel's funeral, a combined service that included words for Buckland and Fitch. Buckland had been buried; Gabriel and Fitch, as penniless wards of the state, had been cremated. So on his first holiday after basic training Joey had come here, to a grotty little stone memorial outside Wentworth, inscribed with the names of those who'd died inside.

Yet even visiting Gabriel, so to speak, was difficult. Joey lingered in the lavatory until he was sure he wouldn't weep. He didn't want to attract attention, didn't want some stranger asking why he was sad.

He located the names easily. The last three: Bertram Fitch, Paul Johnson and Gabriel MacKenna. Fitch's cut throat had been blamed on Gabriel, just as he'd wanted, sparing Lonnie the gallows. The inmates, however, knew the truth – Lonnie Parker, the most unexpected of killers, had put down Fitch. Joey hoped Lonnie's new reputation would protect him, at least for a while. Paulie, who'd enjoyed his freedom for less than a day, had been fatally mauled by a watchdog while trying to steal trousers off an East London clothesline. And Gabriel had bled to death as Joey held him.

Joey accepted the War Office's appointment not to get himself killed, as his friends inside feared, but to reclaim his life. He wanted to survive whatever assignments the SOE gave him, regain a bit of respectability, even rebuild his relationship with Julia, if any shred of their childhood affection remained. And if it all came to nothing, if his number came up during the war, Joey wanted his death to be instant. But if it wasn't, if he lingered, he hoped he endured the spiral as bravely as Gabriel. Joey had felt the other man's pulse gradually flutter and stop, looking into his face as he died. And it had been like gazing on the face of a stranger, someone Joey had never known. Everything that had been Gabriel had fled all at once. Which to Joey meant perhaps Gabriel MacKenna was still intact somewhere. At peace. Or waiting ...

Putting two fingers to his lips, Joey kissed them, pressing them against Gabriel's name. He never knew how long he remained there. Only that some time passed before he turned away, squaring his shoulders and reentering his old life.

THE END

Author's Note

Wentworth Men's Prison, a fictional combination of Wandsworth (where Oscar Wilde was incarcerated) and Pentonville, exists only in my imagination. In most cases, I strove to be accurate, but I took a bit of artistic license with the legal concept known as "irresistible impulse." Diminished responsibility, as we now call it, was still being explored in the 1930s, and I believe it was successfully employed in the United States long before the United Kingdom.

I would like to thank Rosemary O'Malley, J.David Peterson, and the LiveJournal group little-details for their assistance with the research. Also, for this second edition, the wonderful Kate Aaron provided some much-needed feedback. Check out her blog at onlytruemagic.blogspot.com.

A Note Before Coda

Over time, and after conversations with wonderful readers like Julie Small, I decided to add CODA to the book, but as an altogether separate piece instead of an epilogue. If you prefer, consider PROTECTION finished as originally published. Or, like me, you may choose to believe Joey's story only paused, and CODA reveals the true ending.

Coda

By T. Baggins

He'd been walking a long time, most of it over familiar terrain, yet in the way of dreams he wasn't tired. Nor did he question the rise and fall of the landscape, as a symphony might swell one moment and spiral to soft notes the next. So much about his home village he'd forgotten. Born in 1911, Dr. Joseph Cooper had seen tremendous changes overtake Britain in his fifty-seven years. The Great War of his childhood and the Second War in which he'd fought; Britain's replacement as the dominant western power by the U.S.; the sexual revolution and the counterculture. By 1968, London was nothing like the city he'd known in his youth. But the rural villages had changed, too. He'd kept meaning to go back, to have a look, but life always got in the way. Lovely to pass through once more, no one paying him the slightest attention, and soak it all in.

Next he'd revisited Oxford, briefly. It hadn't changed. The towers were still ivory, the professors of Science just as pompous, the medical students just as desperate to excel and be praised. He'd never guessed how crippling the need for approval could be until he lost all hope of it, or thought he had.

After his honorable discharge from the Royal Army, Joey had joined a struggling charity, St. Michael's Hospital in East London. He'd hoped the administrators might permit him to at least step and fetch for the doctors, unload supplies or sweep the floors. But his military record and distinguished service to the S.O.E. had granted him a supervised practice with St. Michael's geriatric patients. After six months, all supervision ceased. After a year, he transferred to the emergency department and quite unexpectedly began making a name for himself.

As he walked, Joey even returned to Wheaton Manor, site of his disgrace. Dr. Pfiser had been dead for ages, but his heirs' threats of legal action had made it impossible for Joey to speak freely in television interviews. Those threats also compelled Random House to withdraw its offer to publish Joey's memoir. That had been fine with him, although St. Michael's –by 1968 one of Britain's most successful charities –was crushed. But Joey had known he'd have to lie or leave out too much for the book to be worth writing. A frank discussion of his conviction would have sparked a legal firestorm.

And any mention of Gabriel would have humiliated his children, not to mention his late wife's family.

It came again, that sound: a screeching, shuddering roar like the end of the world. Joey stopped, listening. He knew the sound but couldn't name it. That, too, was in the way of dreams –effortless knowledge, inexplicable surety. He recognized the sound, knew what it meant. Yet he didn't.

What did it matter? He'd walked hundreds of miles in the course of a day and it all made sense. Just like Wentworth's sudden appearance made sense, looming up in the mid-afternoon sunshine.

Joey remembered his first day at Wentworth. Arriving by bus, he'd shuffled down the steps in leg irons, as he'd recounted for his eldest daughter, Lily, more than once. She'd been both fascinated and terrified by the idea of her father behind bars. Throughout her childhood and teenage years she'd read everything she could find about incarceration and the penal system. Now the knowledge served Lily well as a solicitor. If society ever progressed enough to allow it, she would make an even better judge.

Perhaps it wasn't surprising that Joey's younger children, Stella and Ben, preferred not to think about their father's four years inside Wentworth. But Joey had long since shaken off any shame. In fact, he found himself looking back more with every passing year.

It was noon. Joey glanced around Wentworth's exercise yard, bemused. It should have been filled with inmates. Walking, stretching, smoking, queuing up for the privy. After all, this was the Wentworth of 1936, Joey realized with a smile. Slopping out had yet to be outlawed and Rebecca Eisenberg had not yet helped abolish capital punishment in Britain. In the Wentworth of 1936, the inmates lacked flushing toilets, gymnasiums and tellys. An hour in the sunlight was a treat.

A duck darted out of the watchtower's shadow, quacking at Joey like a watchdog. Bright-eyed and bold, it was clearly someone's pet. He smiled at it, surprised all over again. Surely live animals had never been permitted at Wentworth, not even in cages.

"Oh, that's just Jacky. Never mind him, he's spoilt rotten." Gabriel MacKenna stepped out of the shadows, smiling at Joey. "Well now. At last. Kept me waiting long enough, didn't you?"

"You say that every time," Joey smiled, adoring the sight of this man, his great love even after almost thirty years. "But it's still my favorite dream."

Gabriel came closer. Joey sighed, knowing he'd awaken the moment their lips touched.

"Sweet Jesus. Look at that." Eyes wide, Gabriel stroked Joey's hair, chuckling. "If it weren't so gray you could play Jesus at Easter. Long hair on men. Times have changed, eh?"

Joey caught his breath. Not figuratively, but literally –he felt it, felt his breath stop, felt his heart leap, all the familiar physical sensations of surprise. This was no dream. His body was real. He was real. With a gasp Joey exhaled. Mind racing, he found himself unable to speak, fighting to process the knowledge transmitted by Gabriel's touch.

"Fear not." Gathering Joey in his arms, Gabriel pulled him close. "I always figured there was a reason the angels led off with that. Not hallo, not it's good to be seeing you, but fear not. Because 'fear not' is just what's needed."

"Gabe." Joey was laughing, crying, losing himself in the other man's embrace. And it wasn't fantasy, wasn't a fever dream. Gabriel was real, as lean and compactly muscled as ever, exactly as he'd been on the last day of his life.

"You're alive," Joey said over and over again. "Alive. This is brilliant! More than I ever dared hope! While I've gotten old ... fat..."

"Not fat. Just a wee bit soft right about here," Gabriel grinned, patting Joey's stomach. "Julia kept you fed. T'other one did, too."

"Marc. That didn't last." Joey took Gabriel's face in his hands, staring at him as he blinked away more tears. "He wasn't you. But Gabe, how did you ... how have I..."

The roar came again, the crescendo to an overture, the impact of metal on metal. Not cymbals crashing together. Just an old Packard turning left, trying to outrace an ambulance. And the ambulance driver, a daredevil, infuriated, refusing to give ground...

"Oh, God, we had a patient in the back," Joey groaned, understanding everything in a rush. Perhaps he'd understood from the moment he started walking, but only prolonged the discovery, taking it in bits and pieces until he could accept the whole. "I told Sam his driving would be the death of him –him and our patients, too. Stupid –arrogant –*brainless*!"

Gabriel just stood there smiling, handsome as ever in his prison uniform, the only clothes –outside of pajamas –Joey had ever seen him wear.

"Sam lived. The patient, too. You went through the windshield. Broke your neck. Poor Sam's inconsolable."

Joey felt his anger drain away. That was another change that had come with age; he felt angry rarely and held onto it only with difficulty. What was he always saying to his students, his children, even his patients? "Life is too short."

"Poor Sam," Joey sighed. "I don't suppose I could get a message to him? Tell him I'm all right?"

Gabriel's hazel eyes gleamed. "What do you think?"

Jacky waddled over, quacking imperiously, and Gabriel withdrew a handful of corn from his pocket, scattering it over the yard's scrubby grass.

"Why a duck?"

Gabriel shot him another grin. "Boyhood friend. I told you not to fear. Why are you shy of me?"

Joey sucked in his breath, dazzled by how alive he felt, how bright and real death had turned out to be. "Gabe. You never aged a day. I'm almost sixty."

"Are you?"

The cell was just as Joey remembered it; bunk beds, a small table and two chairs. No toilet, only a steel bucket in the corner. No sink, only a water basin with flannel and a cake of hard yellow soap. A small rectangular mirror was fastened to the wall for shaving. Joey, facing that mirror, saw himself at twenty-nine: ginger-brown hair cropped short, face unlined, eyes still wide and long-lashed. Nude, he was better-formed than he'd ever appreciated in those days, chest and shoulders broad, stomach concave.

Gabriel was hard against him, whispering Gaelic to Joey, once-mysterious words he now understood perfectly.

"I've waited for this. It's been days ... days..."

"It's been thirty years," Joey heard himself reply in Gaelic. But that wasn't right. Even during the busiest times of his career, even when his children demanded all his free time, even in the earliest blush of his affair with Marc, Joey had never been separated from Gabriel for more than a few days. Never in his heart.

Gabriel pulled Joey into the bottom bunk. Their lovemaking was delirious, inexhaustible, unending. He had no idea how long they'd been at it, or how many variations they'd enjoyed, feasting on each other like starving men. But suddenly Joey realized what was missing.

"Gabe. You aren't smoking."

"Don't need it."

"But ... no. In a world where a duck needs corn, Gabriel MacKenna needs a Pall Mall."

Gabriel grinned. "Ah, but I'm different in one respect," he said, tapping his chest. "No part of me hurts anymore."

Gradually Joey realized that no part of him hurt anymore, either. He wanted to worry for St. Michael's, for poor guilty Sam and the often feckless Board of Directors, but he couldn't. He couldn't even worry about Lily, his secret favorite among his three children. He'd loved them well and seen them grow up strong. They might miss their father, but they had no more need of him.

More lovemaking, violent and perfect except for occasional spasms of fear. When they interrupted Joey had no choice but to stop, pull away and shiver, hugging himself until Gabriel kissed and stroked him back to quiescence.

"Why does it keep happening? Why do I get so afraid?"

"Because it's a struggle, putting aside your

humanity. Who you were on Earth. Here there's only happiness, peace and pleasure. That's unnatural on Earth. 'Tis an unnatural state for human beings, we weren't designed for it."

"I have to learn to tolerate heaven?" Joey laughed, surprised.

"There is no heaven. Nor hell, as you told me yourself. Those are just notions for human beings. Not always bad notions. But no more true than planet Earth being borne through the cosmos on the back of a great turtle."

"Then what is this place? Are we here together for eternity?" Joey pressed himself closer to Gabriel. His body no longer was limited by a need for rest; already he wanted to make love again.

"This place is where we come to make the transition," Gabriel said in English, in Gaelic, and in another, inhuman language Joey understood somewhere deep inside. "There is always someone or something here to greet you, to soothe your fears, to help you understand. For you, that person is me."

Joey held Gabriel fiercely, loving him not in body or words but in pure essence. It was a trick he'd learned instinctively, sweeter and more terrifying than mere intercourse. "Oh, Gabe. You were okay, weren't you? You didn't just have Jacky to greet you?"

Gabriel's laughter was bright, brilliant, almost physical. No –it was physical, three-dimension, new and yet familiar. How had Joey failed to perceive that before?

"Of course not. The duck's a pet. 'Twas Vera came to meet me, and stayed with me 'til I was strong enough to wait alone."

Joey thought about that. "You were engaged to Mattie. Your other girl was Sheila. And of course you always fancied Marlene. Who was Vera?"

"In life, she was my mum."

Joey stared at Gabriel.

"We had a lot to say to one another. John and I, too. But when I ready, Vera left. Then John, too."

"Your father?"

Gabriel nodded.

"Where did they go?"

"We can't know. It's not a secret. We simply aren't capable of comprehending, so we receive no explanation. Whatever comes next is unknown, Joey. Vera went into it alone. So did John. They were done with one another, and with me."

"I'm not done with you," Joey said, alarmed, holding Gabriel tighter. Soon they were making love again, at first in body, then more dangerously, merging their essences.

"It's good. Scary, but good," Joey breathed, no longer completely certain where he ended and Gabriel began. It was like the perfect merger of strings, woodwinds and brass into an orchestra, a unified sound far more than the sum of its parts.

"Joey. If you don't choose to go now, soon, you'll miss the chance to go alone."

Joey took that in, bringing their essences close again, afraid and unafraid. He no longer perceived Gabriel in the flesh. And what he saw, he loved even more.

"If we transition together –I don't know what will

happen," Gabriel said. "We may become one."

"If we transition together –I don't know what will happen," Joey said. "We may become one."

They spoke in unison, holding the last word like a single perfect note. And when the sound faded, they did, together.

THE END

About the Author

Orphaned at birth, T. Baggins was raised by wolves until age fourteen, when the pack moved on one night without a forwarding address. Returning to human society, Ms. Baggins taught herself to read and write by studying fan fiction. Cutting her teeth on Kirk/Spock (*Star Trek: The Original Series*, baby!) she soon began slashing rock stars and X-Men. Despite a lifetime spent in the southern U.S., T. Baggins considers herself a citizen of the cosmos and a freethinker, which is good, because no one has offered so much as a penny for her thoughts. In her spare time she enjoys blogging at Shades of Gay, emptying gin bottles and tweeting into the void as @therealtbaggins.

Also by the Author

Fifteen Shades of Gay (For Pay)
Something Different

Made in the USA
Coppell, TX
10 February 2025

45704201R00094